THE BLOOD OF SOLOMON

THE 72 DEMONS

BOOK ONE

JAMES E WISHER

SAND HILL PUBLISHING

Edited by: Janie Linn Dullard

Cover art by: Stone Tower Studio

ISBN: 978-1-68520-066-4

032520241.0

CHAPTER ONE

Daisuke Kugo let out a long groan and stretched. The flight from Switzerland to Japan was a long, miserable one even if you went first class. It would've been so much easier to just shadow walk, but magical entry was strictly forbidden in Japan and he didn't want to get off on the wrong foot after ten years away. At least there was no rule against keeping your luggage in an extra-dimensional space, so he was free to skip baggage claim.

The bathroom, however, wouldn't wait. Merging with the flow of people streaming away from the arrival gates, he made the short walk to the men's room and ducked inside. It was packed, but after a short wait he had his turn then went to the nearest free sink. As he washed his hands he noticed a middle-aged man wearing an ill-fitting suit staring at his right arm. Covered from fingers to elbow in ugly, blotchy burn scars, it certainly wasn't an attractive sight. He usually wore thin leather gauntlets that hid it, but airport security required the gloves be removed.

Unable to stand it any longer Daisuke snapped, "What?"

"Nothing, sorry."

The curious fellow offered a little bow and hurried away, hands still dripping.

Daisuke's outburst had drawn even more eyes his way. No matter the circumstances, you simply didn't make a scene. It was rude. And being rude in public was a grave breach of etiquette. All the old lessons were coming back and he hated each and every one of them. Drying his hands and going outside, he paused long enough to pull his gloves on. If customs wanted them off, he'd remove them when he had to.

It should've been simple for a priest to heal his scars; the nurse at his old school had offered as soon as she saw them. The problem was that they were as much a curse as a burn. Besides, Daisuke would've refused even if healing was possible. They served as a constant reminder that his family—his face twisted in a bitter smile when he thought of those people as family—had cast him out at the first hint of failure.

Well, to hell with them. He'd finish his job and be back in Europe by the end of the week. With any luck he could just avoid them altogether. No doubt that would suit them just as well as it did him.

Thankfully customs didn't force him to take his gloves off and after a quick scan of his passport, he was allowed to enter the country. Now to find a cab and get to his hotel. A hot shower would be most welcome.

At the packed terminal he swung past the vending machines and picked up a box of strawberry Pocky before turning toward the exit. Halfway to the doors, he spotted a man in a white suit holding a sign with his name on it.

Shit. Neither he nor his employer had arranged a limo, which meant his family must've found out he was coming and sent it. The only reason they would do that was because they wanted him to come to the family estate.

And no way was Daisuke going to do that. He pretended not to see the driver and ducked outside. A row of ten blue and black cabs sat parked and waiting to his left. He went to the nearest one and opened the back door.

The driver immediately looked over his shoulder at his new fare. He had to be in his sixties and wore a flat cap scrunched down so low on his forehead it nearly covered his eyes. "Where to?"

"The Continental Blue Hotel."

"I know it. Climb in."

Daisuke did so, settling in to the spotless back seat, and glanced out at the ocean as they left the airport behind. It was a beautiful sight, with the sun glinting off the waves. Kurisato International Airport was built on an artificial island that jutted out into the Pacific Ocean. It was built after World War Three decimated the country. Though to be honest, Japan had come through the war in better shape than plenty of other nations. At this point, North America was basically a mutant- and monster-infested wasteland and mainland Asia wasn't much better.

Of course, the war happened long before Daisuke's time —two hundred years before, as a matter of fact.

He yawned, happy to let random facts distract him from the limo driver waiting for him back at the terminal.

"Where you from, kid?" the cabby asked.

Japanese cabbies weren't exactly known for being chatty, but it seemed he'd found an exception. "Here, by way of Switzerland. You?"

"Here. I retired last year, took the cab-driving job to get out of the house. It was that or the wife threatened to divorce me."

Daisuke dutifully chuckled at the lame joke and offered a silent prayer to any listening archangel that the driver would be satisfied.

"What brings you to town?"

"Business." Maybe a one-word answer would get him to take the hint.

"No kidding. Usually the business guys wear suits and are at least ten years older than you. Must be a laid-back business if they let you wear a t-shirt and jeans."

Keep calm and don't cause a scene. That thought ran through Daisuke's head over and over.

"I'm a freelancer and my customers don't care what I wear as long as I get the job done. It was a long flight, so I'm going to rest my eyes until we get to the hotel."

"Sure, don't mind me. It'll be about half an hour."

Daisuke closed his eyes and silently activated a spell. The cab appeared in his mind just as if his eyes were still open. Japan might be a low-crime nation, but he still wasn't about to trust a complete stranger.

Fortunately, the trip passed without issue and soon enough they came to a stop in front of a twenty-story hotel painted deep blue and gray. A sign over the revolving door read, "Continental Blue."

"Here we are," the cabby announced. "That'll be a thousand yen."

Daisuke passed him a black credit card and a moment later got a receipt, his credit card, and the cabby's business card.

"You need a lift somewhere, give me a call."

"Thanks." Daisuke climbed out of the cab and sighed as it pulled away. If he needed a ride, he'd be sure to find a quieter driver.

He pushed through the revolving door and walked through the lobby to the front desk. He had the whole place to himself, which was unusual. The scattered chairs were empty and there was no one perusing the snack bar.

A chime of the brass bell on the check-in counter brought a skinny little man barely tall enough to reach the computer. He typed for a moment then asked, "Do you need a room, sir?"

"I should have one. Daisuke Kugo."

"Ah, yes sir. Mr. Kugo. We have you in a suite on the top floor. All paid up for the rest of the month." The little man reached under the desk and brought out a keycard. "There you are, sir. Do you have bags? If so, I can call the bellhop."

"I'm good, thanks."

So saying, Daisuke headed for the bank of elevators behind the check-in counter. When he glanced back, he found the clerk punching numbers furiously into the phone. That couldn't be good.

He shrugged and pressed the call button. Looked like he was going to have to deal with his family after all, but if he was right, at least they would have to come to him.

The silent ride to the top floor was a boon to his soul. As someone that spent most of his time working alone out in the middle of nowhere, being surrounded by people and having to talk to them was a chore he'd just as soon foist off on someone else. Pity he couldn't this time.

The keycard said room three and he soon found it. The lock beeped when he put the card in and he pushed through the door. The boss certainly hadn't skimped on his accommodations. There was a king-sized bed in the main room, a queen in another room, a huge bathroom with a tub and a tile shower, and finally a full kitchen. He could move in here and live quite comfortably. It was actually nicer than his apartment in Zurich. Not that he spent much time there.

He pulled his phone out, tapped the boss's number and waited. Three rings brought an answer. "You made it okay?" The boss's voice was a rough, throaty purr. She thought it sounded sexy. Daisuke thought it sounded like she smoked too much. Which she did.

"Yeah, no sweat. Any updates on the job?"

"Despite my warnings, the idiots refuse to take the bronze prison out of the exhibit. It's only one item, a rather plain-looking piece, yet you'd swear I was asking them to set fire to the main display."

"That's not ideal. Any word on the seal?"

"Helena lost it."

"Shit! So not only is the prison not secure but the Blood of Solomon has the seal. That's pretty much the worst possible news. Is Helena okay?"

"There's nothing wrong with her that a day in a healing circle won't fix, but it was close. It's all on you now, Daisuke."

Daisuke let out a long sigh of relief. If the boss was that nonchalant, then Helena should be fine.

"Great. If there's nothing else I need to ward my room and get a shower. I'll scout the museum tomorrow. Did Helena at least say who attacked her?"

"She's not awake yet. I'll let you know as soon as she says anything."

"Thanks." Daisuke disconnected and ran a hand through his hair. Helena was one of their better operatives. If she got taken out, the Blood of Solomon must've sent one of their heavy hitters. And now whoever they'd sent would be on their way here.

There were days he regretted taking the boss up on her

offer to join the Circle of Sorcerers. But then he thought about all he'd done and seen over the last three years along with what he stood to gain in the future. Not to mention what he and the world stood to lose if the Circle failed in its mission.

CHAPTER TWO

Yoshikazu Kugo sat behind the expansive maple desk in his office. A single sheet of paper sat on it. Like everything else in his life, the desk was perfectly organized, everything in a drawer or filing cabinet. An ordered workspace led to ordered thoughts. That was the proper way to live your life. Some people might disagree with him, but they were wrong.

Today, it seemed, his ordered life was about to become disordered. He picked up the paper and read the brief report again. Daisuke's plane had landed safely. After disembarking, he either didn't see or ignored the driver Yoshikazu has sent to pick him up. Most likely the latter.

Given how they parted ways, it was small wonder that his son wanted nothing to do with him. Deep in his heart, where weak sentiment lived, he regretted banishing Daisuke from the Kugo clan and sending him to that Swiss boarding school. Not that he would ever, in word or deed, admit such a thing. Keeping someone rejected by the spirits of fire, even his eldest son, as part of the family would be an insult to the

8

King of Flames that had blessed Yoshikazu's ancient ancestor.

But that didn't keep him from missing the son he raised for thirteen years. Daisuke had been smart and hardworking, kind to everyone, the sort of boy a father would be proud to call his own. At least, any father outside of the Kugo clan.

After leaving the airport, Daisuke had taken a cab to The Continental Blue Hotel and checked into the finest suite on the top floor.

And that was the extent of the report. None of his agents knew why Daisuke had returned. Yoshikazu used to get regular reports from the boarding school, but after he graduated, there was nothing, at least not of any substance. His son had wandered around Europe, doing odd jobs, seeming without direction.

Yoshikazu regretted denying him the purpose that would've come as a member of the clan, but his regret meant nothing. The situation was what it was and nothing would change it at this late date. While he doubted Daisuke meant the clan any harm, he needed to know why he was here.

He pulled his phone out of the desk and dialed Ryo, his younger brother.

Ryo answered after a single ring. "Elder brother?"

"Come to my office. We need to talk."

He disconnected and stood, buttoning the jacket of his white suit and adjusting his crimson tie. There was no real need for a formal greeting. He was on excellent terms with his younger brother, but Yoshikazu was about to give him a command as head of the clan, not make a request as his elder brother, and certain forms needed to be maintained.

A single knock sounded on the door. "Come in."

The door slid open and Ryo's muscular, six-foot frame filled the entrance. He wore a perfectly tailored white suit, polished black shoes, and a black tie. On the right side of his head, just above his ear, a crimson stripe the same color as Yoshikazu's tie ran through his short hair. This wasn't some foolish fashion statement, but a mark from the spirits that signified Ryo's place as the most powerful fire magic user of his generation.

Ryo took one step inside the office and bowed. "How may I be of service, elder brother?"

"Daisuke has returned and he ignored the car I sent for him. Go to his hotel and make it clear he's to come and see me."

"Immediately?"

"No, I'm sure he's weary after the long flight. Tomorrow will be acceptable."

"And if he refuses?"

Yoshikazu swallowed the exhausted sigh that welled up from deep inside. "We'll deal with that if or when it should come to pass. For now, just deliver the message. That I sent you to do it should be enough to make my seriousness clear."

Ryo bowed again, stepped back, and closed the door.

Yoshikazu unbuttoned his jacket and loosened his tie. The rituals and pretense might be necessary for keeping the lives of the four master clans orderly and peaceful, but there were times that even he despised the phony nonsense. Had propriety allowed it, he would've simply gone to Daisuke's hotel and talked to him as his father.

His faint smile was bitter. More likely he'd show up and get the door slammed in his face. That was no less than he deserved, at least from Daisuke's perspective.

Almost no time had passed since his brother's departure before the door to his office slid open again. Only one person in the household would dare enter without knocking. His beautiful wife, Kiyoko, today dressed in a crimson silk kimono and wearing her long dark hair down, stepped inside, closing the door behind her. He had no trouble guessing what brought her here.

"Is it true?" she asked. "Our son is back?"

He nodded and motioned to one of the chairs in front of his desk. When she'd sat he said, "I sent a car for him, but he ignored it. Ryo's gone with an invitation."

"It will be a wonder if he doesn't ignore that as well. We've done nothing to endear ourselves to him these last ten years."

"We did what had to be done, and Ryo is not so easily ignored."

She looked at him with her sad, liquid brown eyes. It seemed every look she'd given him since Daisuke left was sad. "You would have done better to send me."

"You know how that would look."

"Ah, yes, mustn't do anything that might give the incorrect impression. It's only our son we're talking about after all. You will let me see him when he arrives."

That last wasn't a question but he nodded all the same. They needed to keep Daisuke's presence at the estate quiet, but he wouldn't dream of trying to stop Kiyoko from seeing him.

"We'll all see him. Perhaps even a meal, just the four of us. Shogo would like that, I think."

She lowered her head in the tiniest of bows. "He always liked ramen. When do you expect him?"

"Tomorrow. When, I can't say."

"We'll plan for dinner then." She stood and left without another word.

When she'd gone Yoshikazu finally let out the sigh he'd been holding in. How long since they'd told each other "I love you"? He couldn't actually ever remember saying it.

Theirs was an arranged marriage and love had nothing to do with it. Still, after twenty-three years, you'd have thought something might have developed beyond respect.

He suspected any hope he'd had of that died ten years ago.

CHAPTER THREE

A hot shower had been just the thing. Between the flight and setting wards around his suite, Daisuke was all in. Maybe a light snack from room service then bed. He had a museum to visit tomorrow and he wanted to get there before the crowd.

Wearing nothing save slippers and a towel around his waist, Daisuke stepped out of the bathroom only to find someone sitting in one of the chairs that surrounded the dining area table. Even if he hadn't recognized the distinctive red streak in his hair, the white suit and dead, shark eyes would've made it clear who was here. He'd set wards to scare away spirits, but hadn't done anything to keep people away. It was a hotel after all and blasting the cleaning staff would win him no friends.

Besides, he hadn't figured anyone would simply walk in and make themselves at home.

"Ryo, I suppose His High-and-Mightiness sent you since I ignored his driver."

"You'd best show more respect, boy. To both your father and myself."

"I'm not a member of the clan anymore and you're not a cop." He dropped on the bed. "You're due no more respect than any other random person I might meet. Less, considering you entered my room without being invited. Let me guess, you used the Kugo name to bully the desk clerk into letting you in. At least you didn't melt the lock, I guess."

"Are you done?"

Daisuke thought for a moment. Antagonizing Ryo was fun, but he wanted to eat and sleep. The sooner he said what he had to say, the better. "Yeah, I'm done. What do you want?"

"Your father expects you at the estate tomorrow." Ryo stood. "Don't make me come back and tell you again."

It took all Daisuke's self-control not to ask, "Or what?" Ryo was leaving and that was enough for him. He had no intention of visiting his childhood home. There was no one he wanted to see there. Well, it might be nice to see Mom and Shogo, but not nice enough to deal with Yoshikazu.

His childhood felt like another life.

It was, for all intents and purposes.

When the door closed behind Ryo, Daisuke added a sealing ward that would keep anyone else from entering until he removed it.

What the hell did his family want anyway? He hadn't gotten so much as a birthday card in ten years. Now they expected him to jump when they called?

He rolled out of bed and went to the closet where he'd left his neatly folded clothes hanging. From his pants pocket he took a flat steel card engraved with the image of a treasure chest.

Ether flowed into it at his command and when the treasure chest glowed white, he tossed the card in the middle of the bedroom floor. It vanished and an actual treasure chest appeared in its place. Around three feet tall and wide and six feet long, it actually looked more like coffin.

He flipped the lid open and a fat, foot-long rat crawled up out of his clothes. "I thought I was going to suffocate in there."

"You're an imp. You don't even breathe." Daisuke had made a contract with Ruq five years ago when he found the half-dead imp trapped in a cage in the dungeon of an ancient castle he was exploring. He regretted the decision on a semi-regular basis.

"I'm claustrophobic," Ruq said.

"Where did you hear that word? And get off my shirt, you're wrinkling it."

The imp jumped out, putting even more wrinkles in one of his clean black t-shirts in the process. He did it on purpose, Daisuke felt certain.

"I heard it on TV. A commercial advertising something called an open MRI."

Daisuke shook his head and grabbed clean underwear and a pair of pajamas. Ruq was obsessed with television, especially late-night infomercials. The imp claimed he could get humans to sell their souls for nineteen ninety-five as long as he included a free set of steak knives. That was so messed up, yet he couldn't deny there was plenty of truth to the sentiment.

"You hungry?" Daisuke asked.

"Starving."

"Want the usual?"

Ruq's tiny rat head bobbed in a nod. Daisuke grabbed the landline and called in his order. That done, he sat on the bed, picked up his cell phone, and pulled up all the information he could find on the Kurisato Museum. There was plenty of marketing copy, general information about the various exhibits, and... Here we go. A whole page all about the ancient artifacts that would be on display starting this weekend. At least there was no mention of Solomon or the demon prison, not that whoever the Blood of Solomon sent to claim the prison was likely to need a website to find out where it was.

What he really wanted was a complete floor plan, but of course they didn't have one. That would've been too convenient. As usual, he'd have to do things up close and personal.

Someone knocked, hopefully the bellhop with food.

Daisuke opened the door and grinned. A young man held a silver tray with two hot fudge sundaes on it. "I'll take that, thanks."

After setting the tray on a handy table, he returned and handed the bellhop a hundred-yen bill.

"Thank you, sir. Just set the tray outside your door when you're finished."

Daisuke nodded and closed the door. Now for his snack. Ruq had already climbed up on the table, but he knew better than to eat before Daisuke joined him. He sat and put his hands together. An annoyed glance prompted Ruq to mimic the gesture with his little paws.

"Thanks for the food." So saying, Daisuke started eating with one of the ridiculously long spoons that came with the sundae.

Ruq just made his mouth ten times bigger and dove in. To say that the imp had bad table manners would be greatly underselling the display of gluttony he put on, but the ice cream was so good, Daisuke couldn't even be bothered to chastise him.

When they finished Daisuke sighed. "That was delicious."

"Mmm. Could've used a cookie or two, but otherwise I have no complaints." Ruq's tongue grew a foot long and he started cleaning off his fur.

Having seen enough of his familiar's habits for one day, Daisuke picked out a fresh set of clothes for tomorrow then transformed the chest back into a metal card. His work complete, he offered a silent prayer that he could go all day tomorrow without seeing any members of his family, crawled into bed, and soon fell fast asleep.

CHAPTER FOUR

The Kurisato Museum of History and Fine Arts took up four blocks in the middle of Kurisato's downtown business district. Two stories tall and likely a couple levels deep, the museum had six exits that Daisuke had located so far.

I found a roof access, Master. Ruq's voice appeared in his mind. His familiar, having transformed into a pigeon, was keeping an eye on things outside.

Great, seven ways for whoever the Blood of Solomon sent to get in here. Even with a standard team of four, there was no way they could cover every entrance.

By himself? He shook his head. Impossible. It would have to be close security for the opening tomorrow.

Made of stone and glass with a row of columns framing the main entrance, the museum looked out of place surrounded by the more modern steel structures. Cafes as well as stands selling tourist junk surrounded it. A huge banner hung over the entrance advertising the ancient pagan collection of premodern magical artifacts. This weekend only, so don't miss it.

That was a mouthful of bullshit. What they had on display were crude ritual artifacts with no inherent magical properties, a few trinkets worn by millennia-old demon worshippers, and the bronze demon prison. It looked a bit like an urn only sized for the ashes of small dog. There wasn't a bit of external decoration on it save for a circle on the lid that was recessed about a quarter inch with a small rune that identified the demon inside. That was where the seal would fit.

When the two came together, the demon would be freed and forced to serve the bearer of the seal, assuming that person had the correct knowledge to compel its obedience. If they didn't, well, whoever opened it wouldn't live long enough to regret their stupidity.

Having arrived before the museum opened, he was the first one inside. While there was no sign of the actual artifacts, there was a plaque with pictures and a little description. There were no wards in place to protect the artifacts yet. Hopefully they'd prepare some before the grand opening tomorrow. The place had at least one wizard on staff, so the boss said anyway.

That was the person she'd hoped to convince to pull the demon prison. Clearly the wizard was an idiot, which gave Daisuke little hope for whatever protection he put in place.

Leaving the first level behind, he found a set of stairs leading to the second floor. There was a balcony that overlooked the display. That would probably be his best bet for an observation post. If he couldn't figure out where the enemy would appear from, the only other option was to stake out the one place he knew the agent would show up.

He settled on a spot that gave a perfect view of the entire display. From here he could see everyone coming and going. It would help if he knew what the Blood agent looked like, but so far, no word from the boss. That meant Helena was still unconscious or at least in no condition to talk. She must've really gotten messed up.

Satisfied with his scouting, Daisuke made his way toward the main exit. He took a deep breath of summer air. Not as sweet as the Alps by a mile, but interesting in its own way. He ambled over to an open-air cafe and settled at an empty table. It was still early and he was the only customer.

A cute young waitress wearing a hair band decorated with cat ears hurried over, note pad in hand. "What can I get you, sir?"

"Hot chocolate if you have it."

"We do!" she said in a far-too-excited tone. With a bow of thanks, she hurried off to get his drink.

There was nothing else for him to do today and he debated just relaxing at the hotel. But that would be lazy. No, surveying the museum and seeing if anyone suspicious showed up was the thing to do. Technically Ruq would be doing most of the actual surveying, but he wanted to be close on the off chance anyone put in an appearance.

I'm always doing all the work.

Save your whining for someone that doesn't know how lazy you are; I don't want to hear it.

The waitress returned with his hot chocolate and Daisuke took a sip. Delicious, though he would've liked a few marshmallows to go with it.

It took him a moment to realize that the waitress was waiting for him to say whether it was okay or not. He set the mug down and smiled. "It's fine, thanks."

She beamed and hurried away.

So young and enthusiastic. He'd worked at a restaurant once and hated every second of it. Of course, he'd been dead broke at the time and in addition to his meager pay, he got two free meals a day so he'd swallowed his pride long enough to save what he needed for a bus ticket to Romania, where a very promising ruin had drawn his attention.

Those had been the days. Wandering Europe in search of lost magic, battling guardian monsters, defusing wards, generally living by his wits. He'd learned a great deal during those three years after graduation. Sometimes he regretted agreeing to join the Circle of Sorcery. Life was so much more complicated now. Then he remembered the size of the boss's private library and grinned. Unrestricted access to the library between missions was priceless. Plus he couldn't deny a certain amount of satisfaction in knowing that he was making a difference in the world.

There's someone climbing up to the roof, Master.

Show me.

Daisuke closed his eyes and strengthened his link with Ruq. Sure enough a figure in gray coveralls was climbing onto the roof from the fire escape Daisuke had noticed when he walked the perimeter earlier. He or she, it was hard to say from where Ruq perched, carried a tool box making him think maintenance man. But that would be a perfect cover for someone up to no good.

Switch to ethereal view.

The swirling, chaotic flow of ether, the energy field that served as the medium for all magic, appeared. There was no sign of either the worker or anything in the toolbox inter-acting with it. That meant no magic or a caster so skilled they could hide their ability from him.

If someone like that was here, Daisuke was in trouble.

Over the next five minutes, whoever he was watching fiddled with an electrical box on the roof. The worker did nothing suspicious, either magical or mundane, and left nothing behind. Looked like it really was just an employee.

He spent the rest of the day camped out at the cafe, making sure to order both lunch and dinner and to leave a large tip when he left. After the electrician departed, nothing of note happened. It felt like a waste of time, but Daisuke had been at this job long enough to know that waiting and watching was just part of the deal.

Hopefully tomorrow, but maybe Sunday, the real trouble would begin.

Natsumi Kugo stood outside her uncle's office, hands clasped behind her back, and waited. She'd received the call only minutes after getting home from the last day of school and she was still wearing her blue and white uniform. For the past month she'd been hinting that she'd like to do something for the clan this summer, but no one had yet said if her wish would be granted. She was an adult now, even if she did have a year of high school left. There must be some way she could help.

If she was about to get a job, she expected Shogo to be here as well. They were the same age and in the same grade, so if she was about to get an assignment, it stood to reason that he would too.

The index finger of her right hand started tapping against her left wrist and she immediately stopped it. Fidgeting was one of her bad habits and she had to constantly fight it. A

Kugo warrior didn't twitch, play with her hair, or sigh with frustration when forced to wait for the clan leader's attention. She stood, back straight, still and silent until called upon.

She just wished it wasn't so damned hard!

Ten minutes later the door slid open and her father stepped out of the office. His face was impassive and his suit perfectly pressed. He was everything a warrior should be and Natsumi did her best every day to be worthy of his example.

He offered a small nod then marched silently off on whatever errand Uncle Yoshikazu had sent him on.

"Come on in, Natsumi," her uncle said.

She stepped through the open door and bowed. "You summoned me, Uncle?"

"I did. The director of the Kurisato Museum—he's a friend of the clan—has recently been made aware of a threat to steal a rare and valuable relic that's going to be on display this weekend. He asked if I could send someone to help with security."

Her heart leapt. Finally, a real mission.

"There's no guarantee anything will even happen, but he considers the threat credible. I thought this would be a good opportunity for you to get some real-world experience. And if some thieves should be so foolish as to try and steal something under Kugo protection, I'm confident that you'll be up to the task of stopping them."

She bowed. "I won't disappoint you, Uncle."

"Stop by the armory in the morning and collect Flame Edge before you leave."

Her brow creased. Flame Edge had been in the family since their ancient ancestor received the King of Flame's blessing. She'd wielded it a few times in training, but as far as she knew, no one had taken it out of the compound in decades.

Uncle Yoshikazu must've read her confusion. "It's probably overkill for thieves that might not even show up, but better safe than sorry."

"As you say, Uncle." She hesitated. Since this was a formal meeting, personal questions weren't really appropriate.

"If you have something to say, say it."

"Is Daisuke still coming by today?"

Her uncle's stern face turned down in a deep frown.

Natsumi cursed inwardly. She should've kept her mouth shut and focused on the job.

"How did you hear about that?"

"Shogo told me while we were waiting for the bus this morning. He seemed excited to see his bro—" She caught herself in the nick of time. "To see Daisuke again."

"That boy needs to learn discipline. I told him the visit was to be kept quiet. No matter now. He hasn't shown up yet and there's no indication he plans to. A few hours remain in the day, but it looks like he has no intention of accepting my invitation."

"How rude! Who does he think he is to refuse a summons from the head of the clan?"

For just an instant a crack appeared in Yoshikazu's stoic demeanor. But then it was gone so quickly she thought she must've imagined it. "I suspect he thinks he's no longer a part of the clan and that my summons holds no power over him. And officially he's right. But I need to know why he came back. I don't think he's a danger to the clan, but if there's even a tiny possibility that I'm wrong…"

"What will you do?"

He waved her off. "That's not your concern. Focus on your task and let me worry about Daisuke."

Natsumi was well trained enough to know the conversation was over. She bowed again and backed out of the office.

Daisuke must still be holding a grudge if he was willing to ignore his own father. She almost felt bad for him considering what was likely to happen when Uncle Yoshikazu decided to force the issue.

CHAPTER FIVE

The ringing of his phone woke Daisuke from a sound sleep. A glance at the window confirmed that it wasn't even daylight yet. He groped around in the dark until his hand fell on the nightstand and his phone.

"Yeah?"

"Sorry to call so early," the boss said. "But Helena finally woke. I've got good news and bad news."

"That's rare. Usually you just have bad news. Let me have it."

"Good news is, Helena's going to make a full recovery, though she'll be out of the field for at least another week."

"That's certainly better than the alternative. And the bad news?"

"She said two agents attacked her. One a wizard and the other a highly skilled martial artist. The wizard was a man, late thirties or early forties, dark skin, and dressed in an all-black suit. The fighter was an Asian woman. Sounds like he specializes in support magic and she handles direct confrontations. We've got nothing in any of our files about Blood of Solomon agents matching their description."

Daisuke sat up, thoughts of more sleep long gone. "When you have bad news you don't screw around. Are they actually Blood agents or do you think a third party is interested in the prison?"

"I wish I knew. Assume third party until you know for sure one way or the other."

"Right." He ran a hand through his sleep-rumpled hair. "What are the odds of getting some backup out here?"

"If the matter isn't settled in a week, I can send Helena, but other than her, everyone's committed." The boss sounded as tired as he felt.

"We need more people."

"Yes, but it's not like I can just go down to the employment agency and hire them. I can't even hire technical staff that way. We let one wrong person into the Circle and it could jeopardize every agent in the field."

"I know, I know. Can you at least tell me which demon I'm dealing with should the worst happen?"

"Sorry, Daisuke. Helena didn't get a good enough look at the symbol to memorize it, so I can't look it up."

"Grand. Anything else?"

"Just my wish that you have good luck."

"I'll take all I can get. Go to bed, boss. You sound like hell."

"Precisely my plan. Call me tonight no matter what."

"Will do." He disconnected and flopped back down on the pillow.

So he either had two Blood agents to worry about or two unknown third-party players and potentially a different Blood agent that no one knew about. Daisuke had been dealt some shitty hands since he took this job, but this one was right up there with the worst.

He put his phone back on the nightstand and flicked the lamp switch. Squinting against the glare, he rolled out of bed and dug the room service menu out of the drawer.

"You want waffles or pancakes?"

"Yes," Ruq said. The imp had shifted back to his preferred rat form and climbed up on the bed.

Daisuke ordered four of each along with bacon, hash browns, and lots of maple syrup. Not a very Japanese breakfast, but he'd gotten used to this kind of thing during his time in Europe and now seldom ate anything else. He never worried about getting fat. Just maintaining his link to Ruq burned a lot of energy. Three thousand calories was a normal day that he didn't expect to be using magic. Today he'd be wise to double it, at least.

He finished his shower just in time to let the bellhop in with a tray of food. Once the meal was complete, he sat on the floor and closed his eyes. Opening his awareness fully to the ether, Daisuke centered himself and prepared for what he hoped would be an eventful day.

CHAPTER SIX

Daisuke reached the museum ten minutes before it opened and sent Ruq, once more in pigeon form, to watch the outside. A modest crowd had already gathered, including a number of families with little kids. Not what he wanted to see when the potential for an encounter was so high. Ideally he'd prefer to fight in the middle of nowhere, but that seldom seemed to happen. Important as it was to keep the demon prison out of the wrong hands, keeping civilians safe was also a priority.

If you split your attention, you're liable to end up dead.

Your concern is touching.

If you die, I end up back in Abaddon's hell where I'm on rather poor terms with management.

He grinned. That was more like it. Ruq had never said exactly what he did to end up in a cage and on a demon lord's shit list. Daisuke figured anything that made Abaddon mad had to be a good thing for the universe.

The door finally opened and the line streamed in. He didn't even bother with the first floor, instead heading straight to his lookout point. When he arrived and studied the scene, he couldn't decide if his luck was good or bad. There still weren't any wards, but there was a wizard, along with half a dozen armed security guards.

The problem was the identity of the wizard. It was his cousin, Natsumi, and she carried the family katana, Flame Edge. He recognized it at once from the crimson-stained ray-skin wrap around the hilt.

Just like every other member of the family when they were out on business, she wore a white suit. He couldn't help smiling when he looked at her. The reed-thin tomboy he remembered had grown into a beauty at eighteen. She'd be even prettier if not for the serious scowl twisting her features and making deep creases in her brow.

It came as no surprise that she now sported the same crimson streak in her hair as her father. Shogo couldn't be thrilled that she'd received the spirits' recognition as the most powerful wizard of her generation. His little brother and cousin had been competing over everything for as long as Daisuke could remember. She was only eight when he left Japan and Daisuke had no idea if she'd recognize him.

Of all the wizards he might've had to worry about, why did it have to be a member of the Kugo clan?

Maybe you should've gone to talk to them.

If I had, they'd expect me to obey every time they said jump. That's not something I want to encourage. Besides, scouting the museum was more important.

Not that they'd learned anything important, but he hadn't known that to begin with.

Well, whatever. Natsumi might serve as a distraction if nothing else.

He leaned back against the wall and settled in to keep watch. It was going to be a long day, assuming the Blood agents even showed up. Pity a folding chair would've been too obvious.

Every fifteen minutes he shifted his vision to the ether and every time saw nothing save Natsumi's protective magic and the aura of fire around her katana. Lunchtime arrived and the crowds thinned out. Daisuke took a box of Pocky out of his pocket and started nibbling. He would've preferred strawberry, but the vending machine only had cookies and cream.

Halfway through the box a tremor ran through the ether.

Master.

I felt it too. Do you see anything outside?

No, it's all clear.

They must've snuck in with the crowd. He'd pretty much expected that, but would've been pleased to be wrong.

He mentally prepared several spells as he surveyed the crowd. At least there were no kids, thank heaven.

From the second-floor walkway directly across from him, a stunning woman with long dark hair and dressed in all red leapt down to the floor.

"Halt!" Natsumi put a hand on her katana.

The woman in red sprinted forward the instant her feet touched the floor.

Her movements were a blur.

A palm heel strike sent Natsumi flying.

The security guards went for their guns, but they might as well have been stuck in toffee. A flurry of punches and kicks laid them all out in seconds.

But those seconds proved important.

Natsumi recovered and drew her katana. Crimson flames blazed around it as the spirits displayed their wrath.

"This is your final warning," she said. "Surrender or face me."

The woman in red smiled, a barely visible quirking of her lips.

To his left power gathered.

That was what Daisuke was waiting for. He hurled the magic he'd gathered, disrupting the enemy wizard's spell.

Ignoring the raging battle below, he sprinted toward the wizard. When he reached the source of the spell, he found nothing.

Where the hell did he get to?

A pained shout from below prompted Daisuke to spin around, just in time to see Natsumi slam into the museum wall.

Again.

The woman in red went for the prison.

With no other options, Daisuke pointed and black tentacles shot out from the shadows of the display stands.

His shadow binding wrapped her arms and legs, locking her in place.

For a second anyway.

A counterspell virtually identical to the one Daisuke had cast a few seconds earlier smashed his spell to pieces.

He started another, but she took off like a deer from the wolves.

Natsumi sprinted in pursuit, her own body-strengthening magic allowing her to stay close.

Shit.

It was probably a trap, but he couldn't just leave the demon prison behind.

Daisuke leapt down to the first floor, smashed the display open, and slipped the prison into his extra-dimensional storage trunk. It would be safer there than anywhere.

The wizard is waiting in the back alley, Master. I believe your cousin is in trouble.

Of course she was. Typical Kugo. Too arrogant to imagine that there was something she couldn't handle.

Whatever he felt about his family, he couldn't just let her get killed.

Daisuke sprinted for the exit and said a silent prayer that he wouldn't be too late.

Natsumi arrived at the museum half an hour early and went to the rear entrance just as her uncle had instructed. She carried Flame Edge in her left hand, ready to draw it at a moment's notice. Ordinarily, someone walking around with a katana would quickly draw the attention of the security forces, but everyone knew the Kugo clan. Since they were an unofficial part of the nation's military, members of the clan could get away with carrying weapons that would get an ordinary citizen arrested.

With her car safely parked in an employee-only slot, she marched up to the door and knocked. A nervous little man wearing perfectly round glasses, an ill-fitting gray suit, and sporting a thin mustache bowed to her. "Miss Kugo?"

"Correct. You would be Director Waki. My uncle sends his regards."

"I am most grateful that Lord Kugo could send someone on such short notice. One of my colleagues got wind of a threat to the artifact and called to warn me. She suggested not displaying the item in question, but I refused to give in to thieves."

She nodded. Though an unimposing man, Natsumi liked the respect Director Waki showed her uncle and also that he was brave enough not to give in to threats. "What do you wish me to do?"

"Come in and I'll show you."

She followed him through twisting corridors until she was totally lost. They finally stopped in a large room filled with display cases. They held old bits of metal, bone, a horned skull that had to have belonged to a demon, and a variety of other old junk.

"An impressive collection, isn't it?" he said, mistaking her mental inventory taking for actual interest in the items on display. "Everything here is over three thousand years old. The bronze cylinder in case two is the item the thieves are supposed to be interested in."

Her gaze shifted to the item in question. It didn't look like much. The only area of interest was a slight, round depression on the top that was marked with an odd design unlike anything she'd ever seen.

"What is it?"

"We're not certain. There's some magic on it that our resident wizard has never seen before. She intends to study it more closely after the exhibition. All you need to do is stay with the security team. Hopefully, seeing a member of the Kugo clan protecting the artifact will be enough to dissuade any thieves that might show up."

Natsumi nodded again. That would, indeed, be best. There would be hundreds of noncombatants in the museum on a Saturday. If she had to let loose with her fire magic, tight control would be necessary to avoid any accidental injuries. The greater danger was that her opponents wouldn't be as concerned about collateral damage.

A woman in a dark business suit stuck her head in the room. "The stands are all ready, sir."

"Send in the movers," he said.

Eight museum staffers dressed in white coveralls entered the room and gathered up the cases. Natsumi and the director followed along behind them as they made their way to the main floor of the building.

Six armed guards were waiting in the display area. They each kept a wary eye on their surroundings. Their vigilance was a good sign and she felt better about working with them now that she'd seen it.

Introductions were made and the displays set on the wooden stands prepared for them. The whole process took about fifteen minutes. During that time Natsumi made a quick circuit around the room. Four halls led to it and the second-floor balcony let visitors look down at the display. It would also make a good place for a thief to sneak up on them. The space was hardly secure, but what could she expect—this was a public place, not a fortress.

When the preparations were complete Director Waki said, "We open in five minutes. I leave everything in your hands. Thank you again."

He bowed one last time and walked away.

Once he was out of sight and throngs of people started strolling by and through the display, the pressure of "all in your hands" really settled over her. This was her first mission and she was responsible for artifacts that were thousands of years old as well as the safety of hundreds of people. When Uncle Yoshikazu gave her this mission, she'd assumed it would be simple, but the truth was hitting her in the stomach, literally. Natsumi felt like she was going to throw up.

A few slow, deep breaths calmed her. Everything would be fine. She'd been training her whole life for this. She would complete her mission and bring honor to the clan.

The morning dragged on and she found it hard to maintain total vigilance. Her mind wandered as her gaze drifted over the crowd. On the second-floor walkway she thought she saw a familiar face, but then it was gone. Maybe someone from school came with their family.

Her stomach snarled as lunchtime approached. She ignored it. Breakfast would have to hold her until the museum closed and her responsibility was discharged for the day. At least the crowds began to thin.

The moment of relief didn't last. Some strange magic gathered on the second floor. Perhaps the person that caught her eye wasn't so friendly after all.

She spun when it grew stronger. A woman in red, her body crackling with energy, leapt down from the second-floor balcony.

The moment her black sneakers hit Natsumi said, "Halt!"

The woman sprinted forward so fast her body seemed little more than a blur.

A blow to the chest sent Natsumi flying back to slam into the wall hard enough to knock the breath out of her despite the magical protection she'd put in place. Had she failed to take that precaution, a broken spine would've been her reward.

Whatever magic she was using, it wasn't something Natsumi had encountered before. Basic body strengthening wouldn't be enough to overpower Natsumi. She was using that spell herself and was considered one of the best at it.

With an undignified groan, she climbed to her feet.

Just in time to watch the last of the security guards fall.

Natsumi drew Flame Edge and it instantly blazed with crimson flames as the spirit of the sword responded to her will.

Her opponent looked up from the unmoving guard.

"This is your final warning. Surrender or face me."

The bitch actually had the nerve to smile.

Behind her, magic gathered.

Not good.

If she turned to counter the wizard, another trip into the wall would be the least of her problems.

As quickly as it formed, the magic shattered and vanished. Natsumi had no idea what happened, but when the woman in red's smile withered, she assumed it wasn't part of her opponent's plan.

She charged into battle again, just as fast as last time.

But Natsumi was ready and so was Flame Edge.

That made surprisingly little difference.

The finest bladework in the world did you no good if your opponent was too fast to hit.

The woman in red evaded a horizontal slash, spun away from an overhead chop, and lashed out with a side kick that sent Natsumi flying back into the wall.

Her vision went blurry and she felt certain at least a few ribs were cracked.

She tried to get up and failed the first time.

The second try got her to her knees and finally her feet. Ether flooded into her broken and weary body.

When she finally was able to focus, what she saw made her jaw drop. The woman in red was fleeing toward one of the rear exits. A quick glance confirmed that the artifact was still where it was supposed to be.

What the hell was going on? There was no one to stop her and yet she still fled. And where was the wizard she sensed?

Natsumi shook her head. None of that mattered. She couldn't let the thief get away.

As she ran after her, Natsumi's mind raced to come up with a new plan. Much as she hated to admit it, the woman in red had superior fighting skills. That meant she'd have to keep her distance and rely on magic.

Not her preferred way to fight, but certainly doable.

She rounded a bend and found a slowly closing door leading to the alley beside the museum.

Outside the woman in red waited.

"You should've kept running," Natsumi said.

"Why?"

That single word hurt Natsumi worse than either of the blows she'd taken. And she didn't even have a comeback. They'd fought twice and Natsumi got crushed both times.

Well, not this time. She leveled Flame Edge and called on the spirit's power.

A stream of fire rushed out only to splash against an invisible barrier five feet short of the target.

A dark-skinned man in a black suit appeared from behind the woman in red. Even from a distance she could sense the man's power. He was not someone to be trifled with. One-on-one she could probably take him, but the pair were too much for her.

Her body arched as pain unlike anything she'd ever felt ran through her.

It lasted only a second before some other magic negated it. A black disk appeared under the woman in red and inky lightning arced up from it into her body.

A scream tore the air before her partner negated the spell.

Natsumi dared a glance behind her. Another man in black, this one in denim and a t-shirt with pale skin, dark hair, and Japanese features.

"Let's go," the man in the black suit said.

The woman in red snarled at her, ran to her partner's side and the two of them stepped through a dimensional door.

"Not your finest hour, Natsumi."

She spun and raised Flame Edge. Her eyes widened. "Daisuke? What are you doing here?"

"I'm impressed that you remember me. How about you put that sword away and we get you to a doctor?"

She winced. The adrenaline and magic were fading and the pain rising. She sheathed Flame Edge. "We have a healer on duty at the estate and I know Uncle Yoshikazu wants to talk to you."

Now it was his turn to wince.

"Fine. I'll call a cab."

"No need. My car is in the back lot."

She took a step, staggered, and Daisuke caught her. "Easy. You've had a rough time."

He scooped her up and her cheeks warmed. "I can walk."

"You can barely stand." He set out for the parking lot, carrying her like a child. It was the final embarrassment of a day filled with them. "Which one's yours?"

"The red hatchback."

The passenger door opened at his approach. Natsumi hadn't even felt the ether stir. How had a boy rejected by the spirits become so skilled in magic?

He set her gently in the passenger seat, closed the door, and climbed behind the wheel. Daisuke started the car but before he could put it in gear she grabbed his arm.

"The artifact! The bitch must've rung my bell worse than I thought if I forgot about it."

"Relax, it's safe with me. If the idiot museum director had just listened to my boss, none of this would've happened." Daisuke backed up and pulled into traffic.

That statement raised more questions than she had the mental capacity to deal with at the moment. Her uncle and father could handle it. Right now all she wanted to do was rest.

CHAPTER SEVEN

The Kugo estate sprawled across a hundred acres north of the city. In addition to the main house, there were training yards, servants' quarters, storage buildings, apartments for distant relatives that didn't really belong to the main family, and a modest forest where the younger family members played and trained with both magic and weapons. Daisuke had loved it when he was a kid, but those good memories had turned bitter over his ten years of exile. Now he just wanted to do what he had to and get back on the trail of the mystery thieves.

Why not just return to headquarters with the artifact and call it good?

Ruq had turned invisible and slipped into the back seat while Daisuke was loading Natsumi into the front. He glanced at her and found she'd fallen sound asleep. He was grateful as she certainly would've asked questions he didn't want to answer right now.

I'd be perfectly happy to do so. I'll call the boss tonight and see what she wants me to do.

He turned off the main road onto a dirt track that led to the estate. The dirt was every bit as smooth as pavement, probably thanks to Sakani earth magic. The four master clans helped each other out like that all the time. Fire magic was great for combat, but generally useless for anything practical.

When the front gate came into view he slowed and shook Natsumi awake. "Hey, we're here. I need you to tell the guard on duty I didn't kidnap you."

"If you kidnapped me, why would you bring me home?"

"That was just an example. I need you to vouch for me or they won't open the gate. I'm not exactly in good standing with the clan right now."

"Right, right." She rubbed her eyes and yawned.

The gate was actually just a heavy bar attached to a pivot built into a guard house. Further on there was an actual gate made of heavy timbers that let you into the walled-in main compound. It was all remarkably medieval.

The guard on duty stepped out of the shack. He wore the family uniform of a white suit and crimson tie and carried a submachine gun across his chest. As he approached, Daisuke rolled down his window and Natsumi leaned across him. "Hi, Matsu. Would you let them know that I'm back and I brought Cousin Daisuke with me?"

"Yes, ma'am." The guard bowed and returned to the shack without even giving Daisuke a second look.

Not that Daisuke blamed him. He'd happily look at Natsumi all day every day.

The gate went up and Matsu waved them through.

Daisuke grinned as he drove. "I guess everyone still thinks of you as their princess."

"Do not call me that. I always hated that nickname."

"I know, that's what made using it so much fun."

They arrived at the wall and found the gate open and a guard outside waving them through. Daisuke drove into the courtyard and turned right toward the garage.

"Second stall is mine."

He pressed the remote clipped to her visor and parked in the designated spot. To the right was a white limo and the left a red SUV.

"Don't forget the remote."

"Yes, Princess."

Natsumi glared at him, drawing another grin. Daisuke found it somewhat hard to hate someone that had only been eight when he was banished.

She gingerly climbed out of the car and he hurried around to make sure she didn't fall on her face.

Her stride seemed steady as they set out across the yard to the main house. Built in the old style with two stories and a red tile roof, the Kugo mansion looked exactly as he remembered. Old memories came flooding back, most of them good, some less so.

Had he come back five years ago, he would've happily burned the place to the ground and pissed on the ashes. Now he simply didn't care. It wasn't home, just a place he used to live.

The boss told him once that hate didn't make you strong, it only left you hollow and tired. Many bad things would be happy to fill up that empty space. She spoke like the voice of experience, but he hadn't known her well enough to ask for more details. He still didn't if he was being honest.

Halfway across the yard the mansion door slid open and Yoshikazu stepped out. He had a little more gray in his hair and a few more wrinkles, but other than that he appeared exactly as Daisuke remembered from his thirteenth birthday. Seeing the man he'd called father in front of him again brought nothing but emptiness. He might've been a corpse at a funeral for all Daisuke cared.

"I expected you yesterday," Yoshikazu said.

"I was busy yesterday. Natsumi got pretty banged up. How about we take her to the healer then we can talk?"

"I know the way," Natsumi said. "I don't want to hold you up, Uncle."

"You sure?" Daisuke asked. "I had to carry you to the car."

She snarled at him. "I'm sure."

Natsumi limped off, leaving Daisuke and Yoshikazu alone.

"You want to talk on the porch or what?" Daisuke asked.

"My office. When we're done, your mother and brother want to see you as well."

Daisuke slipped his shoes off and followed Yoshikazu inside. "Why? They haven't been interested in me for the past decade."

"It's complicated."

"Right."

Walking through the house felt like going back in time. Nothing had changed. The white walls, minimal decorations, rice paper doors, everything felt like it was out of a historical drama.

They finally reached the office and Yoshikazu waved him inside before closing the door.

Daisuke dropped into an empty chair. "What's so pressing that you sent Ryo to make me an offer I couldn't refuse?"

"But you did refuse. Your mother made ramen in expectation of your arrival."

"I never said I was coming. The rest of the family might jump when you snap your fingers, but I'm not really a Kugo anymore. You made that perfectly clear."

"I told you, it's complicated. Why did you come back to Japan?"

"Business."

"What happened at the museum? Is that more of your business?"

Daisuke blew out a sigh. There were some things he needed to be circumspect about, but most of the Circle's business wasn't that secret, at least not in the magical world.

"You know the artifact Natsumi was supposed to protect? My boss is the one that called in the warning. She wanted the museum director to pull it from the display and turn it over to me for safe transportation back to our vault. He refused. His ego apparently wouldn't allow him to accept that the threat was as serious as he was told. Instead it seems he called you."

"What is the artifact?"

"Do you know the legend of Solomon the Wise and the seventy-two demons?"

"Some of it. It's just an old story."

"No, Solomon was real and maybe the most powerful wizard that ever lived. To secure his kingdom from the lords of hell, he challenged them to a duel. Each lord sent nine demons to battle Solomon, over the course of eight days.

"There are nine lords of hell."

"Since it wasn't happening on or under the water, Dagon wasn't interested. Anyway, the deal was that if he won, the lords and his followers wouldn't trouble Solomon's kingdom for five thousand years. Solomon defeated the demons, but instead of destroying them, he bound them into bronze prisons. That prevented them from being resurrected in Hell to continue spreading evil."

"The artifact is one of these prisons?"

"Correct. The thieves that attacked Natsumi also defeated

a colleague of mine and claimed the seal that will allow them to open it and control the demon inside. Needless to say, that would be a bad thing."

"Where is the artifact now?"

"Safe. As soon as we're finished here, I'll take it to headquarters and put it in the vault. Once it's secure, hunting down the thieves and finding the seal can be done in a more orderly manner."

Yoshikazu leapt to his feet and slammed his hands on the table. It was as powerful a reaction as Daisuke could remember him making. "You stole it! That artifact belongs to the museum and we were hired to keep it safe. If I let you leave with it, our clan will be dishonored."

Daisuke raised an eyebrow then held out his left hand. "Potentially setting a demon loose in Kurisato." He held out his right hand. "A tiny ding in your honor." His hands went up and down as if weighing the words. "Are you really going to compare the two?"

"Without our honor the clan is nothing," Yoshikazu said. "I can't let you leave with the artifact. It will be as safe here as in your vault."

Daisuke finally stood and looked his father in the eye. "Nowhere is as safe as the vault. Are you really willing to risk it?"

"A better question is, are you willing to fight the entire clan to get out of here with it?"

Master, the house has been encircled by several dozen wizards.

"I should've just called Natsumi an ambulance." Daisuke pulled the metal card out of his pocket and summoned his chest. The demon prison sat on top of his shirts. He grabbed it and slammed it on the desk. "Here. Whatever happens, it's on your head."

Daisuke took his phone out and snapped a picture of the

symbol on the top. At least he could have the boss look up which demon they were dealing with.

The wizards are retreating.

"I sense no corruption."

"Of course you don't. Solomon's magic has completely encased it. If someone didn't know what it was, it could easily be mistaken for a simple altar relic or other ceremonial piece. I assume that's what the director was told by his wizard."

Yoshikazu hefted the prison and gave a little shake of his head. "So much fuss for such a little thing."

"Keep thinking that way if it makes you feel better. I'm out."

Daisuke stood and turned toward the door.

"Will you not stay for dinner?"

He nearly laughed but somehow managed to stay polite. "I think not. The thieves are still out there and I have work to do."

"Your mother and brother will be disappointed."

"I'm sure they'll both survive. Good afternoon."

Daisuke slid the door open and stopped dead. His mother waited a few paces away dressed in a red kimono, just like he remembered. For a moment warm feelings came flooding back only to be chilled seconds later. He didn't know how to feel when he looked at her. Anger was easier, but also not completely honest. He'd missed his mother horribly for the first few years of his banishment but eventually sadness turned to rage. And eventually the rage cooled to ambivalence.

Now that they were together again, he didn't know what to feel.

She smiled and held out her arms. "Daisuke. Welcome home."

It took all he had not to completely break down, either in anger or relief. "Hi, Mom."

Natsumi limped her way toward the healer's office. Given their work, the family kept one on hand at all times. This one was a second or third cousin, she couldn't remember. Sako was an absolute sweetheart and had healed Natsumi many times after particularly rough training sessions. She had also tried to heal Daisuke's burns after he failed the ritual, but spirit fire wasn't so easy to heal since the damage had as much in common with a curse as it did an actual burn.

The door to Sako's office was closed, but the red cross sign wasn't out which meant she wasn't with a patient. Natsumi went in without knocking. There were two treatment beds on the right, a workbench and cabinet with medicine on the left. Sako sat behind the workbench, dressed in all white as was her habit. The woman was close to fifty and had a round, soft appearance that everyone found soothing. At least Natsumi did.

Sako looked up and her dark eyes widened. "What happened to you?"

Natsumi sat on one of the beds and winced when her ribs complained. "I had a disagreement with a wall. As you can see, the wall won both rounds."

Sako hurried over, her hands already glowing white with healing energy. She pressed them against Natsumi's back and the pain faded.

"Four broken ribs, cracked sternum, mild concussion, and more minor contusions than I care to count. Want to talk about it?"

"Let's just say I didn't cover myself in glory today. In fact, much as I hate to admit it, had Daisuke not shown up when he did, I'd likely be dead right now."

"Daisuke's back? When did he get here?"

Natsumi shrugged then winced. "Not sure exactly. Day before yesterday maybe. He's talking with Uncle Yoshikazu now."

"I doubt that will be a pleasant conversation."

Since he blew off his father's summons yesterday, Natsumi couldn't help agreeing.

The treatment took only five minutes and when it was over Sako said, "There, all better. I recommend taking it easy for at least two days. I'm not sure why I recommend it since you always ignore me. My optimistic nature, I guess."

"I'll do my best. Thanks, Sako." She kissed the older woman on the cheek and headed for the door, her body no longer protesting with each step.

Outside, leaning against one of the posts that held up the roof covering the walkway was Shogo. Having just left Daisuke, the differences in their appearances were even more obvious. Shogo's features were all sharper, especially around his eyes. He was also a couple inches shorter and a bit less muscular.

"Heard you got your ass kicked." Shogo grinned. "Uncle Ryo isn't going to be happy."

Natsumi shot him a glare out of habit, but there was no heat in it. Even if he was needling her, everything Shogo said was the simple truth. She'd been so confident in her abilities. Strongest of her generation, the spirits proclaimed. And she couldn't even handle two thieves on her own.

"It would've been a lot worse if Daisuke hadn't helped me."

"Big brother's here?" Shogo perked up. "He was supposed to come to dinner last night but never showed."

"Are you surprised? Your dad sent my dad to basically summon him. Anyway, they're talking now."

"It must not have gone well. Dad summoned all the clan wizards to the main house a couple minutes ago before dismissing them."

"If Uncle Yoshikazu is trying to make up with Daisuke, he's got a funny way of going about it. Walk with me to the armory? I've got to return Flame Edge."

"Sure. And you know Dad. That's just the way he is."

They rounded the corner in time to see Daisuke and Aunt Kiyoko walking together toward the garden behind the main house.

Shogo took a step toward the pair before Natsumi caught his shoulder. "Maybe give them a few minutes alone."

Shogo glanced at her then nodded. "Sure."

Natsumi turned toward the armory, but sent a final glance back over her shoulder. She wasn't quite sure what to make of her newly returned cousin. Saving her life had made a good first impression, even if it was kind of annoying. Hopefully they could patch things up. Having the family back together again would be nice.

After a quick hug, Daisuke followed his mother out into the garden. There were gravel paths lined with flower beds, arches with rose vines covering a brook that had a pair of bridges over it, and an air of tranquility that did nothing to settle his nerves. Out of everyone in the family, his mother was the one he was most nervous about seeing again.

"I'm glad you decided to visit," she said.

"I wasn't going to, but I had to bring Natsumi back. Yoshikazu made me turn over the artifact I was supposed to protect. He called me a thief and said it would be a stain on the family honor if I took it somewhere safe. He even threatened to sic the aunts, uncles, and cousins on me if I didn't hand it over."

"You know your father."

Daisuke shook his head. This was the moment he'd been both dreading and needing for the last seven years.

"No, Mom, I don't."

She cocked her head. "I don't understand."

Daisuke stopped and she turned to face him. "After I left, I was obsessed with figuring out why the fire spirits would reject a member of the Kugo clan. As far as I know, that's never happened. I couldn't stop thinking about it. Then one day my senior year, in math class, the answer came to me. When it did, I couldn't believe it so I ordered one of those mail-in DNA tests."

The blood had all drained from his mother's face. Just to be safe, Daisuke guided her over to one of the marble benches scattered around the garden and they sat.

"I'm sure you can guess the result."

"You're only half Japanese."

He nodded. "Half Japanese along with a bunch of Northern European. Since I seriously doubt Yoshikazu has much Scottish blood in him, the truth became painfully obvious. The spirits rejected me because I don't have any Kugo blood."

"It was a one-night stand." She couldn't even look at him as she spoke. "My parents had just told me I was to marry your father in a week. A week! That's how long I had to make peace with the idea that I was to marry a man I'd never met. I was so angry I went out that night, got blind drunk, and ended up in the hotel room of the first good-looking man I met. I didn't even get his name. Obviously I never told your father, I mean Yoshikazu."

Daisuke found he wasn't as angry as he expected now the truth had been confirmed. He felt more confused than anything. "Why not tell him after the test? You must've realized why I was rejected."

"Truly, I had totally buried the memory of that night in the deepest recesses of my mind. I didn't remember that much of it anyway. And who knows what Yoshikazu might've done had I told him. At a minimum you still would've been banished and he might have chosen not to offer you even financial support. It was a mistake, a youthful indiscretion best left in the past. You understand?"

Daisuke frowned. "You want me to keep it secret, to go on pretending that the spirits of fire consider me unworthy rather than just not a member of the clan."

"What difference does it make at this point?" She sounded so desperate it made his heart ache. "You wouldn't be accepted anyway. Letting the secret out now would only increase the pain for everyone."

His frown turned up into a smile, a bitter, humorless one. "There was a time, not that long ago, that the idea of increasing the pain of every member of the Kugo clan would've been enough for me to post the truth to social media for the world to see."

"And now?" Her voice trembled when she spoke.

"Now I don't care about the clan. I'm honestly surprised you care since you were basically given to them as a gift by my grandparents." He blew out a long sigh and sent the bitterness and anger with it. They were useless emotions anyway. "If you want to let him go on thinking I'm his son, fine. I won't say anything. As soon as my business is complete, I'll be leaving Japan and if I never have to return, that would suit me perfectly well."

"Daisuke." She reached out to him.

He took her hand and kissed her cheek. "I know it wasn't your fault. I'll never love the clan for what it did to both of us, but I will always love you."

Daisuke held out his arm. "Ruq!"

His familiar, now in the shape of a crow, flew down and landed on his arm. "Goodbye, Mom. I don't know if we'll see each other again, but I'm glad we had this time together."

So saying, Daisuke walked over to the darkest shadow he could find, that of a thick hedge not far from the bench, and vanished into it.

He appeared in his hotel room and dropped onto the bed, emotionally exhausted. His emotions were all over the place and he hated it. Just being angry at all of them was so much easier. "That was why I didn't want to visit my family."

Ruq transformed from a crow to a rat and hopped up on the bed beside him. "Families aren't a thing in Hell. We all serve the will of Abaddon while striving to rise in his esteem."

"Consider yourself lucky." Daisuke pulled out his phone and sent a text to his boss with the symbol attached. "I'm going to take a shower and see if I can wash the bad taste out of my mouth."

"You might have better luck by brushing your teeth."

Daisuke smiled. "It's a figure of speech."

The imp wasn't stupid, so he figured Ruq made the poor joke in an attempt to cheer him up. What did it say about his life that he had a closer relationship to a demon than his own family?

Nothing good, he felt certain.

CHAPTER EIGHT

Itsuko's whole body hurt, especially where that black lightning had struck her. Cristo's dimensional door had carried them to a parking lot a mile from the museum where they'd left their car for a quick getaway. It was supposed to have been a quick getaway with the prison, not them fleeing with their tails tucked between their legs.

She sat on the hood and cursed the universe.

"Do you require healing?" Cristo asked in his deep, sonorous voice. If the whole black magic warlock thing didn't work out he'd have a bright future as a singer.

She thought for a moment then shook her head. Everything hurt, but nothing felt damaged. "What the hell happened? You were supposed to deal with magic."

"Daisuke Kugo is a powerful necromancer. I believe I could take him one-on-one, maybe, but I couldn't do so while maintaining your enhancements. Could you have defeated the girl without my magic?"

"Doubtful." It pained Itsuko to admit that, but the brat

was good enough she had no real hope of beating her with just her natural ability. "What are we going to do now?"

"Return to the apartment and make plans for our next attempt. As long as we have the seal, I can find the prison. The only thing that's changed is the location we need to attack. Nothing less than the demon's power will save us from the Blood of Solomon's wrath."

The sound of approaching sirens prompted Itsuko to slide off the hood and climb in the passenger side of their nondescript tan sedan. Cristo got behind the wheel and they set out for the inn outside the city that they'd chosen for their temporary base.

"Did we make the right decision?" she asked.

"That's a rather broad question."

"Ditching the Blood of Solomon and going off on our own. We both knew what their reaction would be. We could've just turned the seal over and had a nice payday."

"I'm weary of serving others. With the demon's power, we can start our own group or take over one of the smaller cults. We'll be real players in the magical world, not mercenaries and thieves."

"Assuming we can find it before one of their agents finds us."

Cristo flashed his perfectly white teeth. "That was always the gamble. Our first roll of the dice came up snake eyes. Perhaps our next roll will be more successful."

She barked a humorless laugh. "How many rolls do you think we'll get?"

"I wish I knew." He pulled onto the highway and sped up.

The traffic wasn't bad and twenty minutes of driving brought them to their off-ramp. The worst of Itsuko's pain was gone, but she still felt weaker than usual.

"What kind of spell did he hit me with?"

"Black lightning. It's a negative energy spell that burns away your life force with each hit. A couple more seconds and it would've reduced you to a lifeless husk."

"Nasty. I guess he didn't plan to capture us."

"No, that isn't Daisuke's reputation. Nor the Circle's for that matter. People that oppose them tend to disappear, permanently."

"Sounds familiar."

"Indeed, though I'm sure if you pointed out the similarities between them, both the Blood of Solomon and the Circle of Sorcery would hasten to deny such a thing existed. Both sides of this war are remarkable hypocrites."

Cristo touched the brakes and pulled into a gas station. She glanced at the dashboard. They still had over half a tank. "What's up?"

He parked by the station. "Someone just set off the alarm spell I placed on our room at the inn."

"A maid?"

"No, I specifically asked for no maid service today. I fear our former employer has tracked us down."

"That's not good. But if it is a Blood agent, would they have noticed your alarm spell?"

"I used a variation that's very difficult to detect specifically for this reason."

Itsuko nodded. When it came to magic, she'd never gone wrong trusting Cristo. "So what do we do?"

"I had hoped to wait a day to let you fully recover, but it seems we'll need to accelerate our schedule. If you're up to driving, I'll locate the prison and we'll grab it tonight."

"I'll be ready."

Haakon Lybeck scowled around at the empty room. He'd tracked the traitors to this place, an inn situated in the middle of nowhere, but it seemed he'd arrived too late once more. It had been his task to oversee the mercenaries hired by the Blood of Solomon to retrieve the seal and prison. It would've been bad enough if they simply failed to complete the mission. The betrayal had been far worse. Especially since he'd seen no indication of it beforehand.

Itsuko and Cristo had lowered his standing in the eyes of Lord Solomon and the only way to get that back was to kill the pair and complete their mission himself. And he would do this. There was no question in Haakon's mind. Their betrayal had been a temporary setback, not a failure.

Whether his master saw it that way or not was another matter.

A final search through the room yielded nothing to either his magical or mundane sight. He also had to assume that his targets would know that he'd entered and would therefore not be returning.

It seemed he was back to square one.

Haakon stalked out and turned toward the parking lot where his too-small rental car waited. At six foot six and two hundred and twenty pounds, most cars were too small for him, but it seemed every car in this country was designed to make him uncomfortable. That did nothing to improve his already poor mood.

He encountered no one on his way back to the parking lot, lucky for them. As he reached for the handle his phone rang.

It had to be something important since only Lord Solomon and some of the other higher-ranking members of the society—Haakon disliked the name "cult"—had access to his number.

"Yes?"

"The prison has been located," an unfamiliar voice said.

Haakon frowned. That was fast. If one of their agents had found it, that meant the traitors either failed to claim it or hadn't made their move yet.

"Tell me everything."

The stranger did so. Apparently the thieves failed in their attempt to seize the prison though they did manage to kill a number of security guards. A member of the Kugo clan and another unknown wizard had defeated them but the pair escaped.

Though partly disappointed, he was also pleased to still have a chance at killing them himself.

"The prison is being held for safekeeping at the Kugo estate. Itsuko and Cristo will know this as well. If the luck of our ancestor is with you, they may show up and you can claim both the seal and the prison at the same time."

The ancestor's luck hadn't been with Haakon since the day he first laid eyes on the two thieves. Perhaps it was time for that to change.

Out of curiosity he asked, "How did you learn this?"

"Yoshikazu Kugo called the museum director to let him know that the prison was safe. We've had the director's phone tapped since it became clear they had one of the bronze prisons."

Haakon accepted this without question. Given the wealth and power at the society's disposal, such a thing would be no challenge at all.

"I will make my move tonight."

CHAPTER NINE

Daisuke emerged from the bathroom clean in body and still troubled in mind. Not as bad, but he feared the conversation with his mother would be with him for a while. Like, the rest of his life. Why did life have to be so complicated?

He'd barely taken a step toward his pajamas when his cellphone rang. It was the boss's number and he answered it at once. "Hey, boss. Tell me you have some good news."

"I wish I could. The symbol in the Book of Wisdom indicates that it belongs to Vorgon."

"Well, shit. Unless my memory is faultier than usual, that's the name of the elder demon sent by Narukami Tempest."

"There's nothing wrong with your memory, unfortunately. Vorgon is easily one of the most powerful of the imprisoned demons. He was Narukami Tempest's ace."

"Great. So what kind of damage are we looking at if he gets loose?"

"Think of the most powerful hurricane you can imagine,

now double that and picture it covering all of Japan. Now, instead of rain, imagine demon spirits falling from the clouds. That demon must not be freed."

"Okay, so how about you pull some strings with the local government and have them order Yoshikazu to give me the prison. I can have it in your hand in fifteen minutes."

"It's not that simple." The frustration in her voice came through loud and clear.

"The situation or the solution?"

"The solution. I have no contacts high up in the Japanese government, and even if I did, they tend to be prickly about their sovereignty. Not to mention excessively proud of the four master clans."

Daisuke started pacing. Why did everything have to come down to egos and dick measuring? "So basically even if there was someone you could call, they'd trust the Kugo clan to handle the situation anyway."

"Exactly."

"Okay, then what do you want me to do?"

"You know what you have to do, find the thieves and claim the seal before they get the prison. Fighting the Kugo clan isn't something I can ask you to do."

"I couldn't beat the entire clan even if you did ask me to. If I wait until Monday, most of them will be out of the estate on jobs, but even then I'm uncertain how many I'd be dealing with. If it's just Yoshikazu and Ryo it would be a tough fight unless I went full dark side and fought to kill. Whatever I might think about my... the people that exiled me, I'm not willing to go that far. I don't suppose you've got a lead on the thieves."

"I put out feelers, but nothing yet. Somebody has to know them, the question is whether I know the people that do."

Daisuke grinned. "You know everyone, boss."

"I wish that were true. It would make this job so much easier. Good luck, Daisuke. If I learn anything else, I'll be in touch."

She hung up and he tossed the phone on the nightstand. He had no leads and no idea where to start looking. The fight, not to mention his conversation with his mother, had left him exhausted. "I need something sweet. What do you say?"

"Have I ever turned down something sweet?" Ruq had an even bigger sweet tooth than Daisuke, which was saying something.

He called room service and ordered sundaes and cookies. That done he flopped on the bed and turned to look at his familiar. "Do you like desserts because I do or have you always liked them?"

"I've always liked them. Though they were rather hard to come by in the Cult of Abaddon. Food was a secondary consideration to burning sacrifices alive for our lord's glory. I vastly prefer working with you."

So he was a better boss than a demon lord? Daisuke would take his wins where he could get them tonight.

The crack of gunfire woke Natsumi from a deep sleep. Her still-recovering body complained as she dragged herself out of bed and ran to the nearest window. Figures were running around the courtyard and at least one of the outbuildings was burning.

More flames roared through, giving her a better look at what was happening. Three wizards were trying to blast a huge blond man carrying an ax that glowed with a golden light. He was surrounded by armor of the same color and wore a helmet with horns sticking out the sides. He looked like someone who hadn't really studied history's idea of a Viking.

Whoever he was, he had to be insane to attack the Kugo estate on his own.

The thought had barely flitted through her head before the Viking surged forward and sliced a Kugo wizard in half.

Her heart leapt into her throat, but the intruder was just getting started.

He dodged more flames and swung his ax a second time, killing the central wizard.

A flaming arrow shot in, striking him square in the chest.

The Viking shrugged the spell off like it was nothing and cut down the final wizard.

Natsumi's heart raced and her stomach churned. She'd seen enough. Her family was dying and she had to do something to help.

She slipped out of her pajamas, dressed, and ran for the door and opened it just in time to see her father coming down the hall.

"Is that one of the people you fought?" he asked.

Natsumi shook her head. "I've never seen him before."

"It can't be a coincidence that he showed up the same night as the artifact. Stay here, I'll help deal with him."

To hell with that. "I'm good to go."

"You are not. You will stay here. Even at full strength I'm not sure you'd be strong enough to fight this opponent."

Before she could argue more, he ran off toward the main entrance.

Natsumi didn't really think about disobeying. Much as she wanted to help, she knew her father was right. Not wanting to watch the fight from her window, she went to find Uncle Yoshikazu. If anyone knew what was going on, he would.

She passed half a dozen relatives on her way to her uncle's office. The faces she passed looked utterly terrified but also determined. Fear wasn't something the average Kugo felt on a regular basis. Having experienced it for the first time in her life just recently, she worried about her clansmen.

The door to her uncle's office was open and he sat behind his desk, arms crossed. In front of him rested the artifact she'd been assigned to guard.

"Dad went out to fight."

He nodded. "I know. The spirits told me. You should get to the shelter with the other noncombatants."

"I can't just hide. Let me help you."

"I'm not asking you to hide. I want you to help Shogo protect the children and those who can't use magic."

Natsumi shifted her gaze to the artifact. "He's after that thing."

"I assume so. Daisuke warned me that whatever happened would be on my head." Yoshikazu's lips twisted into an expression she couldn't read. "I thought he was being dramatic. After all, who would be stupid enough to attack the estate of the most powerful master clan?"

A voice bellowed so loud that it hurt Natsumi's ears. "Pathetic fire wizards! Bring me Solomon's prison and I will let the rest of you live. Defy me and your worthless clan goes extinct this night!"

"How can he fight us all, much less win?" Natsumi asked.

"I don't know. The spirits are giving us their best, but the flames can't pierce his armor. Get below. You can't do any good here, but if worst comes to worst maybe you can save the innocents from my arrogance." Yoshikazu reached into his desk drawer and pulled out a card. "Take this. When it's over, call Daisuke and tell him what happened. If we lose the prison, it will be up to him to recover it."

She took the card. It said, "The Continental Blue Hotel," and there was some contact information. There was no way she'd need it, but Natsumi slipped it into her pocket anyway. "Good luck, Uncle."

The underground shelter was below the kitchen and she ran that way. As soon as she entered she spotted Shogo standing guard outside the walk-in freezer. When he noticed her he slumped in relief.

"Do you know what's going on?"

"Not exactly." Natsumi told him what little she knew. "Your dad asked me to back you up. I wish I had Flame Edge."

"I'm sure someone got it out of the armory, and they need it more than we do. Everyone's inside. We'd best seal it up."

She nodded and followed him into the freezer. A trap door in the floor was open and they descended. Natsumi closed the door behind her and channeled ether into the ward that would lock and hide it.

Hopefully this protection spell would prove more effective than the clan's fire magic.

Haakon's energy ax slammed into the chest of an enemy wizard, cutting him nearly in half. A faint tickle of heat warmed his back.

He spun and threw the ax. It tumbled end over end before splitting the skull of the wizard that had attacked him. Assuming you could call these weaklings' magic an attack. Were they truly one of the master clans? Everything he'd read before entering Japan suggested the master clans were the pinnacle of magic in the country.

As far as Haakon was concerned it felt like fighting children.

A surge of ether drew his attention toward the main building. Another man in a white suit stood facing him. He held a sword that blazed with blue flames and a determined scowl twisted his features. Perhaps a worthy opponent had finally appeared.

No words were wasted.

Haakon charged toward the newcomer and swung his ax.

Energy blade clashed against blue flame. His opponent didn't even flinch back a step. Looked like he had a talent for body strengthening as well as spirit magic.

Haakon grinned under his helmet. A real fight at last.

The blows rained down fast and furious with neither man gaining an advantage.

Haakon's ax had no weight, so he could swing it for hours without a problem. The real issue was the gnats that kept singeing his back. They couldn't actually hurt him, but the constant attacks were draining his energy. He could only maintain the flow of ether to Erik's Helm for so long and if he ran out of power before his task was finished, only an ugly death awaited him.

Though given his options, dying at the hands of these weaklings would be preferable to returning to Lord Solomon in defeat. The society's master wasn't known for his forgiving nature.

Blue flames roared at Haakon's face.

He slid under them and swung at the swordsman's legs.

The man leapt easily over the slash, just as Haakon wanted.

Gathering himself at a speed that seemed all out of

proportion for his size, Haakon leapt, slamming his shoulder into the man's gut and driving the air out of him.

He skidded across the dirt.

Haakon didn't hesitate.

An overhead chop hacked off the arm clutching the troublesome sword.

Grabbing him by the neck, Haakon lifted the man to his feet and held him with one arm. "Back, worms! If you wish him to live, get back!"

The jets of flame fell silent and Haakon finally turned toward the main house. He dragged the swordsman along with him. He was close enough that he could sense Solomon the Wise's distinct magic.

He followed his magical senses unerringly to a modest office where a single man waited behind a nearly empty desk. The only thing on the desk was the demon prison.

At last.

Haakon tossed the one-armed wizard toward the desk. He landed like a boneless sack, dead or unconscious Haakon neither knew nor cared. All that mattered was the prison.

"Give it to me and I will spare the rest of your clan."

The man stood and walked around the desk to face Haakon directly. This had to be the clan chief, which probably also meant he was the strongest wizard on the estate. Not that such a designation meant much given how weak the rest of them were. The man had guts at least, Haakon respected that if nothing else.

"Who are you?"

"My name is none of your concern. Stand aside or die like the rest of the gnats outside. I swear that if you fight me, I'll kill every man, woman, and child in this compound."

Haakon watched as the chief wrestled with his duty to

protect the artifact versus his duty to his clansmen. At last he stepped aside and motioned toward the prison.

"Take it, but know that this isn't over. The Kugo clan never forgets an insult and you will answer for this one."

Quick as a blink Haakon drew back and hammered his fist into the chief's chest, sending him flying across the office to slam into the wall. He was still alive. Haakon always kept his word and despite the pathetic threat, he had stepped aside.

He collected the prison and turned toward the door. Half of his mission was complete. Now he just needed to find the seal and the demon's power would belong to the Blood of Solomon.

"I'm glad we decided to observe the compound for a while before making our move," Itsuko said as she stood beside Cristo on the branch of a tree overlooking the Kugo estate.

Her partner offered a silent nod before making an adjustment to the farsight spell that allowed them to see the battle raging in the courtyard half a mile away. Their contact in the Blood of Solomon, Haakon, was making mincemeat out of Kugo fire wizards while working his way inexorably toward the main house.

"His magic is every bit as impressive in person as the stories claimed," Cristo said. "Though spirit magic is certainly the best matchup for him given its focus on direct elemental attacks."

"Think you could take him?" Itsuko asked.

"Not in a straight-up fight, but if I caught him by surprise, probably. It would likely leave me in a coma for a couple days though."

"What if I helped?"

Cristo shot her a side eye. "Despite your considerable skill and even with my enhancement magic, you'd have no hope of breaching his armor. And don't let his size fool you, Haakon is exceedingly fast. One mistake would see you bleeding in two pieces on the ground."

"I was afraid you'd say that."

The battle below progressed and one of the fire wizards actually gave Haakon a decent fight. At least he did before losing his arm to a swipe of Haakon's glowing ax.

When he finally emerged from the main house, Haakon had the prison in his hand.

"So how are we going to get it from him?" Itsuko asked.

Cristo offered a thin smile and ended his spell. "Very carefully."

CHAPTER TEN

Natsumi stood at the foot of the basement stairs and listened for all she was worth. The explosions and crashes had ended a couple hours ago, but everyone was still reluctant to unseal the trapdoor. The carnage she'd witnessed certainly made her hesitate, especially given that the youngest members of the clan were down here.

Her little cousins were crowded around their mothers, trembling and looking afraid, but remaining quiet. No sound would escape the ward, but Natsumi appreciated the silence all the same. Given how worried she was, a bunch of screaming kids would've pushed her to the edge.

Aunt Kiyoko stood and came to join her and Shogo. "It's time."

Natsumi looked up at the trapdoor then back. "Are you sure?"

"We can't hide down here forever. There might be injured that need our help. The battle appears to have ended. Open it."

"Do you think Dad's okay?" Shogo asked.

Natsumi had been wondering the same thing, but so far, she'd kept her worry to herself. At least she hoped she had. Given how sharp Aunt Kiyoko was, she'd probably seen right through her.

"I'm sure he's fine, sweetheart."

Natsumi climbed the steps, listening one last time, and pulled the ether back out of the lock. She pushed the trapdoor open and led the way out. There were distant voices, but no shouts or explosions. That was a good sign.

She turned back. "Looks okay. Everyone can come up. I'm going to find my dad."

When no one complained, Natsumi jogged out of the kitchen and turned toward Uncle Yoshikazu's office. If plans needed to be made, that's where she'd find everyone. She passed no one on her way and when she stepped through the open door, she stopped dead in her tracks. There was a huge bloodstain on the floor and it looked like someone had tried to smash through a section of the wall.

If the guy with the glowing armor made it this far, he must have beaten her father. Her throat tightened and her heart raced. The idea that he might lose to anyone never really crossed Natsumi's mind. He'd always seemed invincible to her.

She slipped outside and ran toward the voices. Fire spirits turned the night into day as they flew around above the carnage. Her clansmen were busy in the front yard, some carting injured people toward the healer's office and others carrying bodies that had been hacked into multiple pieces somewhere out of sight.

She'd never seen something so horrific.

Sparing no thought for anything else, she raced for the healer's office. The stretcher bearers she'd seen earlier were waiting outside on the walkway. Through the open door bodies were visible. They covered the floor of Sako's area. The healer herself looked like she'd fought a war. Her usually pristine white dress was covered in blood and sweat plastered it to her back.

She was currently bent over an injured woman, her hands glowing with healing energy. Much as Natsumi wanted to know where her father was, interrupting Sako now would help no one.

Instead she turned to the uninjured lead stretcher bearer, a third cousin she thought, that Natsumi had never been formally introduced to.

"What happened?"

"It was a nightmare. The blond giant went through us like we were nothing. Fire magic bounced off him like it was nothing. Even Lord Ryo with Flame Edge lost to him."

Natsumi let slip a pained gasp.

"Spirits forgive me. I shouldn't have said that."

She shook her head. "Did my father survive?"

"I don't know. He lost his arm in the fight then the giant dragged him into the house. I was busy cauterizing wounds when the invader came back out, but I caught a glimpse of him before he vanished into the forest. He had something in his free hand, couldn't tell what. Your father and Lord Yoshikazu were brought out on stretchers. Whether they lived or not, I can't say."

"Next!" Sako shouted.

Her third cousin offered a nod in place of the proper bow and helped carry his burden into the office.

Natsumi wanted to collapse, but couldn't until she knew for sure whether her father still lived. She squeezed her fist until her nails cut into her palm. She had no idea what it would take, but somehow she'd make that big blond son of a bitch pay for this.

"Natsumi!" Shogo called.

She took a deep breath and turned to see Shogo and Aunt Kiyoko coming her way. Had they heard what happened? Since they were running toward the healer's office, she had to assume so.

"Are Dad and Uncle Ryo okay?" Shogo asked.

"I don't know yet. Sako is still healing the injured. She's working on the last one now."

"I spoke to the bearers that brought them here," Aunt Kiyoko said. "Both men were alive when they picked them up, though badly injured. Your father lost an arm and Yoshikazu suffered multiple broken bones and internal injuries. The man I spoke with didn't have extensive training as a healer, but he figured out that much."

The pain in her chest eased a little. "If they were alive when they reached Sako, I'm sure they survived."

"What are we going to do now?" Shogo asked.

Natsumi pulled the card her uncle had given her before sending her to safety. "Uncle Yoshikazu told me to contact Daisuke if things went wrong. I'd say this qualifies."

"What can my brother do?"

"Against that monster, I have no idea, but at the very least I suspect he knows a great deal more about what's going on than we do."

The pained groans from the healer's office finally stopped and a wobbly, bloody Sako stepped outside. The three of them hurried over, almost as much to catch her if she fell down as to get an update.

"They're both alive," Sako said before she could even ask a question. "Ryo lost a ton of blood and would've died if the spirits hadn't cauterized the stump of his arm."

Natsumi swallowed hard at the word stump, but held herself together.

Seemingly unaware or more likely too exhausted to care, Sako continued. "Yoshikazu had serious internal injuries and numerous broken bones. I've done temporary repairs and stabilized them both, but it'll take weeks at least before either of them is back on their feet."

"What about the rest of the clan?" Aunt Kiyoko asked.

Natsumi was ashamed to admit she hadn't even thought about the others. Only her father's health interested her.

"Eight fatalities and six that I'm not sure will last until morning. Five more with serious but non-life-threatening injuries. A few others with bumps and bruises they got while running away. Given what I've seen, I couldn't even work up the anger to yell at them. You're welcome to go in and see them. I need to grab a couple hours' sleep. I couldn't control the ether now if my life depended on it."

Sako stumbled off toward her room and Natsumi followed her aunt and cousin into the healer's office. Her father lay on the lefthand bed and her uncle on the right. She was forced to tiptoe around unconscious relatives who were relegated to the floor. The office was a horror show and she felt certain she'd have nightmares, assuming she could ever get to sleep again.

Natsumi sat on the edge of the bed and brushed a bead of sweat off her father's forehead. He looked so pale and weak. "I'll get him, Dad. I swear."

Flame Edge sat on the bed beside him and Natsumi helped herself to the sword. It wouldn't do any good here after all.

She stood. "I'm going to talk to Daisuke."

"I'll go too," Shogo said.

"It's three in the morning," Aunt Kiyoko pointed out. "You're unlikely to get a warm welcome if you wake him at this hour."

"Do you think we have time to wait?" Natsumi asked, her tone sharper than she intended.

"I think," Aunt Kiyoko said with infinite patience, "that Daisuke isn't feeling especially friendly toward us as it is and if you barge into his room in the middle of the night, he's liable to kick you out and tell you to handle the problem yourself. He owes us nothing and made it pretty clear that whatever happened to the clan didn't interest him in the least."

Natsumi ground her teeth so hard she feared they might break. A few hours really wouldn't make that much difference, but she couldn't help feeling that every second she wasted was letting the man that killed so many members of her family get that much further away.

"Does Daisuke really hate us that much?" Shogo asked.

Aunt Kiyoko stroked his hair. "Imagine how you'd feel had you failed the initiation ceremony five years ago, got banished from the only home you've ever known, then didn't get so much as a text message from the people you believed loved you more than anything. Then imagine ten years later the people that abandoned you showed up at your door asking for help at three in the morning."

Shogo winced and when she said it like that Natsumi had to admit she had a point. Daisuke had already saved her life once, she could hardly just show up and start making demands.

"I'll wait until six. In the meantime, I'm going to see if I can figure out where the blond guy went."

"Be careful," her aunt said.

"I will." Natsumi set out, more to be moving than because she thought she'd find anything. If her father wasn't strong enough to beat him, Natsumi had no idea how she'd manage it.

But there was no question in her mind that she would.

CHAPTER ELEVEN

Someone banging on his hotel room door woke Daisuke at the unholy hour of six o'clock. He had no wakeup call in and anyone that actually wanted to kill him was liable to blow the door clear off its hinges rather than just knock aggressively.

"Whoever it is," Ruq said. "Murder them quickly so we can go back to sleep."

Daisuke doubted he'd be getting back to sleep now. Or murdering anyone for that matter. He rolled out of bed, scratched his head, and yawned before padding over to the door and looking through the peephole. What the hell was Natsumi doing here?

He opened the door to the extent that the safety chain would allow. "Why are you here? After the day we had yesterday, I figured you'd be sleeping until noon."

"Can I come in? What I have to say is best not discussed in a public hotel's hall."

"If I say no, is there any chance of you leaving?"

"No."

"That's what I figured you'd say." He debated just slamming the door in her face and praying, but if she was here and in such a state, something serious must be on her mind. "Just a sec."

He closed the door, unhooked the chain, and opened it all the way. A quick glance confirmed that none of the other guests had stuck their heads out for a look. Though if the front desk didn't get at least a few noise complaints he'd be shocked.

"So what's up?"

"We were attacked last night. Ten killed, Dad and Uncle Yoshikazu are hanging on by a thread."

Daisuke got a sick feeling in the pit of his stomach. He'd warned Yoshikazu not to keep Solomon's prison. "The artifact?"

"The artifact!" She rounded on him and stuck her finger in his face. "That's the first thing you ask about? Not how your mother and brother are?"

"Princess, if that prison is opened and the demon set free, we'll be talking about deaths in the six-figure range if we're lucky. I assumed that since you didn't mention Mom and Shogo, they were okay."

Her frown didn't go away, but she did lower her finger. "Oh. I guess that makes sense."

"You want to give me some details?"

"It was a new guy that attacked us. He was big and blond, wore glowing armor that our magic couldn't penetrate and wielded a matching ax that cut people in half like they were made of ice cream."

"Did he have a Viking helmet with horns sticking out of the side?"

Her jaw dropped. "You know him. How?"

"I only know him by reputation. His name's Haakon and

he's a heavy hitter from the Blood of Solomon. His helmet is an artifact called Erik's Helm. As long as you feed ether into it, it protects you from any kind of direct attack. The ax is made of the same energy and as you saw it's very effective."

"Even Dad couldn't beat him."

"I'm not surprised. Haakon is a melee specialist. The artifact combined with high-level body-enhancing magic make him virtually unstoppable for as long as he can maintain it."

"So how do we beat him?"

"We don't. In a straight-up fight, you wouldn't last five seconds and I wouldn't last ten. The only way to stop Haakon is to rope-a-dope him and even then you need the correct equipment and location. I don't have the equipment or the bait I'd need to draw him into the right location. I'm going to have to work around him. The important thing is getting the seal before he finds the thieves. As long as he doesn't have the seal, the prison is just an exceedingly dangerous paperweight."

Natsumi shot him a look that implied she wanted to strangle him. "You can't be suggesting that we let him get away with attacking the estate."

"I'm not suggesting anything. I know I can't beat him. And if Ryo couldn't take him, what chance do you think you have? Your skills are just a less polished version of his. Look, I appreciate you letting me know what happened. Why don't you head home? I'm sure they could use your help."

"Oh, I'm going home and you're coming with me."

Daisuke cocked his head. "Why would I be coming with you?"

"Because your mother told me to bring you back."

"Why?"

"What do you mean, why? Your father is on the verge of

dying. I assume she wants you to have a chance to see him one last time just in case."

Daisuke seriously doubted that was the reason, but he had no interest in discussing his family issues with Natsumi. "I'll have to take a rain check. I'm expecting a call from the boss soon, hopefully with a lead on our mystery thieves. As soon as I learn something, I've got to move. Go home and be with your father. Yoshikazu has Mom and Shogo, I assure you he won't miss me at all."

Natsumi clenched her jaw and looked ready to launch another salvo in the argument. Thankfully his phone rang, sparing him the need to listen.

"Morning, boss. No, you didn't wake me. We've got another complication."

"That's not what I was hoping to hear, Daisuke."

"You and me both. Haakon's here and he took the prison."

"How? I thought it was at your family's estate."

"It was. He cut his way through them then walked back out with it. Sounds like a real mess up there. Anything on the thieves?"

"You sound surprisingly calm given that it was your family that got attacked."

"You know better than that, boss. So, the thieves?"

"Right, after jumping through a few hoops, I got access to the museum's security cameras. While I couldn't find a good shot of the man, the woman was another matter. I ran her through our database and got a hit. Itsuko, no family name listed. Also no magical ability."

"The name sounds Japanese. She a local?"

"No idea, it's a fairly common name. Though he didn't get caught on camera, she has a known associate named Cristo Duhaney. He's a nasty character, a warlock dedicated to the sin of greed. The pair earned a name for themselves as mercenaries over the last three years. There're few details, but from the sounds of it, they're not squeamish about their methods."

"Great, so where do I find them?"

"No clue. Crystal's working on a backdoor into Kurisato's camera network. Once she uploads a facial recognition program, we'll get a line on them soon enough."

"I hope so. With Haakon in the mix, time is not on our side."

"If we can't find them, Haakon won't be able to either."

"He's got the prison, remember? It's connected to the seal. If he's got a hound as well, he could be on their trail right now."

"Shit! I didn't even think about a hound. I'll tell Crystal to step on it. Be ready as soon as she finds anything."

"I will be. Good luck, boss."

The connection went dead and he tossed his phone back on the nightstand. A quick shower and some food would do him a world of good. Trying to save a country on an empty stomach never ended well.

He turned for the bathroom and found Natsumi in his path. Daisuke had been so focused on the current crisis he'd nearly forgotten she was here. "I need to get ready. Are you leaving or what?"

"Not without you. I told you, Aunt Kiyoko said to bring you back."

"If it was something important, Mom would've just told you and had you pass it along. Now, if you want to join me for breakfast, that's fine, but right now I need a shower." He brushed past her and closed the bathroom door behind him. Hopefully she'd be gone when he came out.

Natsumi stared at the closed bathroom door and did her best not to burn it to ash. Why was Daisuke being so stubborn? It made no sense to her. Surely after all this time he could let bygones be bygones. Uncle Yoshikazu really could die. Surely he wasn't so angry that he'd risk not having a chance to say goodbye to his own father.

Then again, she thought about what Aunt Kiyoko said to Shogo and wondered how she would've felt had her father banished her from the clan then refused to speak to her for ten years. Since she couldn't imagine such a thing happening, it was impossible for her to say.

Regardless, her task was clear. If she had to drag him kicking and screaming, Natsumi would get Daisuke back to the estate.

"We want three orders of pancakes, three orders of waffles." She spun at the sound of the unfamiliar voice to see the biggest rat ever talking on the phone. "Bacon, hash browns, hot chocolate, and lots of maple syrup. And don't forget the marshmallows this time."

The rat hung up and looked at her. "He forgot to order before jumping in the shower. You distracted him."

"Who? What?" Natsumi had trouble making sense of her own questions. Why was there a talking rat in Daisuke's room?

The rat, fortunately, seemed to understand what she was getting at. "I'm Ruq, Daisuke's familiar. You might want to sit down. You look faint."

That suddenly seemed like an excellent idea. Natsumi settled in a chair at the dinner table. The rat ran over and climbed up another chair to sit right on the table itself. Sitting on its hind legs looking at her, the rat, Ruq, appeared too intelligent to be a real rat, even if it was a familiar.

The silence started to grow awkward, so she said, "I didn't even know Daisuke had a familiar."

Ruq cocked his head in a perfect imitation of Daisuke. "Why would you?"

He had a point, but she was still annoyed that Daisuke hadn't said anything. Why that annoyed her she was less certain. Maybe because it made her think he didn't trust her. Looking back on it, that was probably the truth.

"Um, could you help me convince him to come home with me?"

"Why would I try and convince my master to do something he clearly doesn't want to do?"

The rat's questions were getting on her nerves. That meant she was getting impatient and her father always said she made bad decisions when she got impatient.

"Because his mother asked him to?"

"Interesting. A remarkable number of people seem to suddenly care about him. I assume because you need him to help deal with the current threat." Ruq put one of his paws to his chin as if deep in thought. "But that makes no sense. Daisuke wants to deal with the thieves anyway. There's no need for you people to get involved at all. In fact, if you hadn't, none of this would've happened. Upon consideration, I've decided not to help you. Clearly you and your family are more hinderance than help to the mission."

"I'm going to wring your scrawny rat neck!"

Before an actual fight could break out, the bathroom door opened and Daisuke walked out wearing only a towel. Natsumi stared at his lean, well-muscled body and reminded herself that he was her cousin.

"Why are you naked?" she asked.

"Forgot my clothes. Besides, the towel's covering the best part."

"I ordered breakfast, Master."

"Thank you." He went to the closet, collected some clothes, and turned back to the bathroom. Before closing the door again, he asked, "Did you decide to join us?"

"Ruq ordered enough for three people, so I guess I might as well."

He nodded and closed the door.

"Judging from your crimson complexion and elevated heart rate, I assume you're thinking about having sex with my master."

"I really am going to strangle you."

Half an hour later, stuffed with so many carbs all she wanted to do was go straight to sleep, Natsumi stood up from the table. "So are you coming with me or not?"

She expected him to dismiss the question out of hand but instead he said, "Sure. But as soon as the boss calls, I'm gone."

If he was willing to give her that much, Natsumi would take it as a win. They went downstairs and got in her car. She'd lost track of the rat, but assumed it was still around somewhere. As she drove north, Natsumi kept darting glances at him. The quiet was nerve-racking, but she couldn't think of anything to say.

Half a mile from the hotel she finally blurted out, "What's a rope-a-dope?"

He stared at her for a moment then grinned. "It's a boxing expression from the mid-nineteen hundreds. It means to fight defensively and let your opponent tire themselves out before you move in for the kill. The only way to beat Haakon is to last long enough for his control to slip. Once his armor is down, he's no harder to kill than a normal man. Well, a massively muscled and exceedingly well-trained normal man anyway."

"Sounds simple."

"You think so? After what you saw?"

She winced. He had a point.

"The problem is, despite being a muscle head, Haakon isn't an idiot. When he gets close to his limit, he has no problem running for his life and trying again another day. A good rule of thumb in this line of work and life in general: the game is only over once you're dead. A friend of mine taught me that."

"Where is he now?"

"She, and her game is over. Some kind of weird magical poison killed her two years ago."

"I'm sorry."

He nodded. "In this job, death is never far away. The sooner you make your peace with that, the better."

Now it was her turn to smile. "That is a very Japanese sentiment. Fight every battle like you're already dead and you will know no fear."

"That's a stupid sentiment. I'm very well acquainted with fear and that's saved my life more than once. I prefer, 'A man's got to know his limitations.'"

"Bushido?"

"Some old movie I was watching a few years back. It seemed like good advice all the same."

She shook her head. Before she could ask any more questions, his phone rang.

"That was fast, boss. Where? Got it, I'm on my way." He disconnected and turned to her. "The thieves were spotted at a gas station. Are you going to drive me or drop me off?"

"I owe that bitch a beatdown. Give me the address."

CHAPTER TWELVE

Daisuke checked his seatbelt and held on to the overhead grip for dear life. Natsumi was currently racing along at considerably more than the posted speed limit. Judging from the many angry honks that greeted their passing from the other drivers, her methods weren't winning any friends. Anxious as he was to reach the gas station where the boss spotted Itsuko and Cristo as quickly as possible, he also wanted to arrive in one piece.

Why did you agree to ride with this insane female?

It seemed like a good idea at the time.

His phone rang, offering a welcome distraction. "Boss?"

"They just left the gas station and are heading east. We're tracking them through the traffic cam network."

"Let me know when they stop. We can't exactly fight them in the middle of the street." He turned to Natsumi. "They're on the move. You can slow down for now. The boss will let me know when they get wherever they're going."

A siren sounded behind them. Well, it was only a matter of time.

"Get me the red tag out of the glove box."

He opened it and found what looked like a crimson book-mark on top. Before he handed it to her, he spotted the kanji for the family name written on top.

The motorcycle cop pulled up beside them and motioned Natsumi to pull over. She slapped the bookmark against the window.

Daisuke couldn't see his eyes behind the cop's dark sunglasses, but suspected they were wide. The cop offered a salute and backed off. Natsumi cracked the top of the book-mark and hung it from her rearview mirror like it was a disabled parking tag.

Seeing his expression she said, "The Kugo clan is part of the city's defense network. As long as I have that, no one will bother us. We actually help more with fire rescue than anything else."

"Right. I keep forgetting just how plugged-in the clan is."

His phone rang again. "Boss?"

"We've got another problem."

Of course they did. It seemed there was always another problem. "Let me have it."

"Looks like we weren't the only ones looking for Itsuko and Cristo. Local security forces had a BOLO out for them as well. Three police vehicles are in pursuit."

"You're right, that isn't good. Can you convince them to back off?"

"How many times do I have to tell you that I don't have a direct line to every government official on the planet?"

"Easy boss, I was just asking. How do you want me to handle it?"

"You're on the ground, use your best judgement. We'll try to keep track of them on this end."

"Got it, boss, and thanks for the heads-up."

"What's going on?" Natsumi asked.

"Some cops are about to have a really bad day."

After ten hours of rest, Haakon had finally recovered full control of his magic. The weak fire wizards hadn't been all that challenging, but the encounter had lasted nearly ten minutes and that was getting close to his limit. He'd honestly expected more from one of the vaunted master clans.

He'd returned to the safe house his master made available to him immediately after recovering the prison. The small three-room house at the edge of the city was far from the Blood of Solomon's finest safe house, but it was private and secure. Since Haakon was operating on his own, he had plenty of room. The only downside was the lack of servants forced him to do his own cooking. Luckily it took little skill to sear a rare steak and that was his preferred meal.

Now, full of protein and well rested, he knelt on the floor in front of the narrow bed and started to draw. He used the glowing tip of his finger to inscribe a circle along with a pentagram and runes. When that was finished, he put the prison in the center and charged the runes with ether.

When the final rune started to glow he chanted, "Hunter. Seeker. Hound. You are summoned. Find the key that opens this lock."

Light rose out of the runes and took on the form of a glowing dog. The magical construct sniffed the prison then the air and pointed left just like a hunting dog out of an artist's portrait. The spell was working properly, good.

He snatched the prison out of the circle and headed for his car. The hound followed along at his heel, floating a foot off the ground. The next-nearest house was a hundred yards up the road and hidden by a tall hedge. Just as well since the sight of a floating golden dog would've drawn attention he didn't need. As would a dead neighbor.

Haakon squeezed in and the hound sat in the passenger's seat, once more in a proper pointing position. The annoying part of this process was his inability to go in a straight line. If he could just go where the hound pointed, it would've been so much easier.

Oh well, every hunt had its tedious portions. If this had been an easy job, Lord Solomon wouldn't have sent Haakon to carry it out.

Country roads quickly gave way to crowded city streets. It was still relatively early and the morning work rush was well underway. That slowed his already miserable progress to a crawl. Haakon snarled at the car inches in front of him as if his anger could make it move more quickly.

A fireball would get it moving, but the resulting panic would only slow him further, along with bringing down the wrath of the local security forces.

The hound was holding steady and would continue to do so for twelve hours. If he hadn't completed his task by then, he'd have to wait a full day to summon it again.

They crawled along for fifteen minutes before the hound started to turn and point a little more north and east. That had to mean he was getting closer.

Haakon forced his way across traffic and took a side street into the city proper. He drove slowly, his concentration divided between the road and the hound. When it turned back east again, he took the next side street between a pair of apartment buildings.

They were almost directly ahead of him now.

The scream of sirens approaching made him wince. They

couldn't be after him; no one knew what kind of car he was driving. That likely meant they were after Cristo and Itsuko. Dragging the seal out of a Kurisato evidence locker was more work than he was looking for. Though he could do it no problem. Their guns had no more hope of penetrating his magical armor than the wizards' fire magic.

A fireball shot into the air and an explosion rang out.

Haakon grinned. It looked like the traitors didn't plan on going down without a fight. If the idiot police could pin them down long enough for him to arrive, that would be all the advantage he needed.

Finding the thieves was turning out to be considerably easier than Daisuke had feared. Between the explosions, pillars of flame, clouds of smoke, and crack of gunfire, everyone in the city probably knew where they were at this point.

Natsumi had put her foot to the floor, once again making him doubt the wisdom of traveling with her. On the plus side, every other car on the highway had either gotten off or made an extremely illegal U-turn. As long as the civilians were moving away from the crazy people hurling magic, he didn't care if they broke every traffic law in the books.

They were half a mile out from what sounded like a war when he asked, "Are you ready for this?"

Natsumi flicked a glance his way and slowed when a wall of cop cars appeared ahead of them. "You're damn right. I've got a feel for her moves now. No way is that bitch going to get the best of me again."

Daisuke nodded, but had his doubts. Natsumi might have good fundamentals and technique, but she lacked experience in actual combat. Training was fine, but there really was no substitute for fighting someone that wanted to kill you.

Directly ahead of them a cop was standing in the middle of the road. He started to raise his hand then turned it into a wave, probably when he noticed the Kugo symbol in the window.

"Stop and find out what's happening."

Natsumi looked like she wanted to argue, but the tightening around her eyes vanished as soon as it appeared. She touched the brake and rolled down her window. "What's the situation?"

"We have two criminal wizards trapped in a restaurant parking lot. Thank heaven they weren't open yet. We've been exchanging fire with them but our bullets are worthless." Another explosion interrupted the discussion. "Their fireballs, on the other hand, are highly effective. It's good that you showed up so quickly, Miss Kugo."

"We do our best." Natsumi rolled up her window and pulled away. "What do you think?"

"Sounds pretty standard. Ordinary cops are no match for even a weak wizard, which Cristo certainly isn't. S.O.P. is to keep them pinned down until your wizards arrive or you get enough guns to overwhelm whatever protective spell the wizard is using."

"We can take them together, right?"

"If you can handle Itsuko, I'm pretty sure I can beat Cristo. I say pretty sure because I have no real idea just how strong he is. All we can do is our best. If worst comes to worst, we fall back and make a new plan. Keeping the seal and the prison apart is all that matters."

They reached a double row of cop cars forming an arch in front of the restaurant parking lot. There was a single, bullet-riddled car in the lot. Three of the front row of cop cars had been reduced to blackened scrap.

One of the officers noticed them creeping closer and hurried over. Natsumi switched the car off and they got out.

"You shouldn't be here. Didn't that idiot stop you?"

"I'm Natsumi Kugo and this is my cousin Daisuke. We're your reinforcements."

The cop went from angry to relieved in a heartbeat. "Thank the spirits. Can we leave this in your hands?"

She glanced at Daisuke who said, "Do you have snipers?"

"Our rifles are every bit as ineffective as small arms."

"That's not what I asked."

The cop winced. "Sorry, sir. Yes, we do have a sniper."

"Take me to him."

Before they could move, the ether swirled and a fist-sized fireball came streaking in.

Daisuke pointed and a tentacle of ether lashed out, slicing the spell in half, and making it fizzle away in a shower of sparks.

The cop was staring at him prompting Daisuke to snap his fingers. "Focus. The sniper?"

"Right, this way."

Their guide led them to the far side of the formation where a man that looked a great deal like Ryo crouched behind a car. A bolt action rifle with a large scope and bipod sat on the ground beside him.

After introductions the sniper said, "I put a round right between each of their eyes and they didn't even flinch. I'm not sure how I can help you."

"Ruq." His familiar shimmered into view, now looking like a raven. "This is my familiar. He's going to stay with you. You shoot what he says, when he says. I don't care if you think the target is stupid. Just do it. Clear?"

The sniper grabbed his rifle and set it on the car hood. "You're the boss. If I can see it, I can hit it."

"Good enough. I'll need the rest of you to hold your fire until I say otherwise. I don't want my allies wearing down my protective barrier with stray shots."

The crack of pistols and submachine guns fell silent as the ceasefire order went out.

He debated pulling out his trump card just to be sure, but decided he didn't need it yet. Daisuke turned to Natsumi. "Ready?"

She nodded and they walked between the two rows of cars straight toward the thieves. When they'd put ten yards between themselves and the cops Natsumi said, "You really sounded like you knew what you were doing."

"I do know what I'm doing. Dealing with shit like this has been my job for three years. I usually have more experienced backup with me, but you have potential, so I'm at least somewhat optimistic that things will work out."

"Kiss my ass."

He grinned but it didn't last. Cristo and Itsuko stepped out from behind the car. Neither of them had so much as a hair out of place despite the fifty pounds of lead that had been thrown at them.

"Turn over the seal and we'll let you walk away," Daisuke said.

"The hell we will," Natsumi said.

"Save the country first, remember?"

"Unlike us," Cristo said, "it seems you and your partner aren't on the same page. Given our difficult position, I'm willing to part peacefully."

Daisuke shook his head. "Not with the seal."

"Then it seems combat is inevitable."

As if that was the signal, Itsuko sprinted toward them at magically enhanced speed.

Natsumi rushed forward to meet her.

The two men stared at each other as the women clashed. Daisuke had to trust Natsumi to handle her business alone. A second's loss of focus and he'd be in trouble.

"How long are you going to make me wait?" Cristo asked.

"That's my question. Unlike you, my partner isn't draining any of my power to maintain her enhancement spells. The longer I wait, the weaker you get."

"Despite your youth, it seems you're not a fool. More's the pity."

An inky-black blast shot from Cristo's eyes.

Daisuke deflected it up and out of the way. "That was just sad."

Cristo's calm veneer finally cracked as he bared his teeth and growled. "I will not be mocked by a child!"

Both his hands popped up and a many-times-more-powerful burst of dark energy blasted out of them.

A black disk appeared in front of Daisuke and the blasts vanished into it. "That's more like it. Good to see—"

Daisuke's taunt was cut off when Haakon exploded out of the front of the restaurant. The giant Norseman went straight for Cristo, glowing ax raised. Following along behind the Blood agent was a golden dog wholly focused on Cristo.

So he had a hound spell, just as Daisuke feared.

Cristo scrambled away from Haakon, avoiding a slash that would've bisected him in the process.

Itsuko broke away from Natsumi and rushed to help her partner. What, exactly, she imagined she could do against Haakon, Daisuke couldn't imagine.

Natsumi made to chase her opponent, but Daisuke caught her arm. "This is not a fight you want to get in the middle of."

"We can't let them get away."

"Not only are we going to let them get away, we're going to help them."

Natsumi stared at him like he'd lost his mind. He didn't care. They couldn't beat Haakon and if the only way to protect the seal was to let Cristo escape, then so be it.

Itsuko kicked Haakon in the back hard enough to crush rock and he acted like he hadn't even felt it. Impressive as always. Daisuke had kind of hoped he'd lost some of his touch, but it didn't seem so.

While the three of them were fully engrossed in their lethal game of tag, he focused on the hound. Ether gathered in his hand and he hurled it at the spell. It shattered into glowing motes.

Haakon looked away, just as Daisuke had hoped.

No fool, Cristo used that moment to open another dimensional door.

Shoot the woman in the shoulder, now!

The sniper rifle cracked once and a little puff of blood burst from Itsuko's back just as she and Cristo vanished through the door.

Daisuke grabbed Natsumi's hand and sprinted to get out of sight.

Haakon slowly turned toward the gathered cops and roared at the sky. Frustration radiated off him in waves. Daisuke knew just how he felt.

"Hold your fire," Daisuke said. "Give him no excuse to attack."

"Do you think he needs an excuse?" Natsumi asked as they crouched behind a burned-out squad car.

"His objective is the seal, not us."

As if reading his mind, Haakon turned and ran back through the ruined front of the restaurant. Daisuke wiped the sweat from his forehead. That's what he was hoping for, but he didn't know for sure if Haakon would do the smart thing.

"We're in the clear." Daisuke stood. "Come on."

He walked back to the thieves' car, keeping a close eye on the ground. It had to be around here somewhere.

"What was the point of all that?" Natsumi asked. "They all got away."

"True, but no one died on our side and neither party claimed the other's artifact. Once Haakon showed up, that was the best we could hope for. Here it is."

He knelt beside a dark, wet patch on the ground. It was the blood that had sprayed from Itsuko's wound. He passed a hand over it several times, gathering up as much as he could in a bubble of ether. There wasn't more than a few drops, but it would be enough for what he needed to do.

"See, Haakon can't cast the hound spell again for a full day." Daisuke showed her the blood he'd collected. "We, on the other hand, can begin the search far sooner."

"Is that why you wanted the sniper to be ready?"

"Yup. The dimensional door spell takes a lot of power. I was hoping if he tried to use it, it would weaken the protections he put on Itsuko. Happily, I was right."

"So what now?"

"Now you carry out my mother's orders and bring me to the estate. There's a full magical workshop there and I need to prepare the blood and a tracking spell of my own."

CHAPTER THIRTEEN

I tsuko staggered against Cristo then the light of the dimensional door overwhelmed him. A moment later they were standing in an alley half a mile from the scene of the battle. He could hardly believe his rotten luck. First the cops shot out their tires, then the two from the museum showed up, and finally Haakon barreled into the chaos.

What the hell else could go wrong?

With a groan, Itsuko slumped to the ground, a hand clamped to her right shoulder.

"Are you okay?" he asked.

"I got shot. What's the big idea letting the shield expire like that?"

"I needed the extra power to get us out of there. I assure you, Haakon would've done far worse." Cristo knelt. "Hold still and move your hand."

The bullet had gone straight through, taking a fair-sized chunk of flesh with it. His power had many uses, but direct healing wasn't one of them. And if he didn't get her healed, she'd be useless the next time they ran into the Kugo brats. It was hardly a surprise that Daisuke would be working with his relatives, but it annoyed him all the same. Fire spirit magic was a good deal less of a threat to him than Daisuke's more flexible skills.

"How did that big bastard even find us?"

"A seeking spell of some sort. Since he has the prison, it wouldn't take much to track the seal."

"Does that mean you can find where Haakon is keeping the prison?"

"It does. But right now we need to focus on getting your shoulder fixed and acquiring transportation."

"I'm all for that."

Cristo straightened. "I'll handle it. Stay here."

She leaned back and rested her head on the side of the nearest building. "Where do you think I'm going to go?"

He smiled and walked deeper into the alley. At the rear of the buildings was a dirty parking lot shared by two buildings on either side of the block. Four cars, none of them remarkable in any way, sat packed in the lot. He chose a tan minivan simply because it was the first one he reached, and waved a hand in front of the lock. It popped open and he pulled the handle.

The most shrill, painful car alarm he'd ever heard went off.

The back door of the nearest building slammed open and a man dressed in a white cook's apron emerged with a rolling pin in his hand. His red face was dusted with flour and he glared at Cristo through narrow eyes.

"Get the hell away from my car!" The baker waved his rolling pin like it was a sword.

Finally, Cristo's luck was turning. "Do you have the keys?"

"What I've got is a beating and I'm happy to give it to you." The baker charged down three steps and rushed toward Cristo.

Dark energy gathered around his hand and he hurled it at the baker.

The unlucky fellow went rigid as the paralysis spell took hold.

Cristo walked over, his right index finger crackling with black lightning. "I asked you a question. Do you have the keys?"

No reply. Most people shit themselves when confronted with real magic. Just his luck he'd run into someone brave.

He ran his finger down the baker's cheek, burning a line in the flesh. At least, it looked like burning. What his magic actually did was rot the flesh away. The pain was excruciating, as Cristo well knew, having tasted his long-dead master's ire from time to time.

The baker's scream was cut off by a gag of magic.

When Cristo finished his first line, he removed the gag. "The keys?"

"My right front pocket."

"That's much better." Cristo retrieved the keys and slipped them into his own pocket. "This is going to hurt a bit."

"Wha—" The gag reappeared, muting his pointless question.

Cristo began a life drain spell. As the baker's life energy slowly gathered in a glowing golden ball beside him, his body withered.

For Cristo, healing someone was an inconvenient, two-step process. Direct healing was much simpler, but as a warlock dedicated to the sin of greed, he couldn't give, only take. Normal healing required the person casting the spell to transfer a portion of their own life force, magnified by ether, to heal the target of the spell or, if they worshipped one of the archangels, to channel divine energy. His magic simply wouldn't work that way. He had to take from someone else and use that.

When the spell finally ended, the baker collapsed into a pile of gray ash. Cristo nodded to himself and walked back to where Itsuko waited. Golden energy flowed into her and her body regenerated until there was no sign of the injury.

"Better?"

"Much. What now?"

"I got us a car. Now we find a safe place to hole up. We need food and sleep. Then I'll trace Haakon through the seal. He has to sleep sometime. When he does, we sneak in and claim the prison."

"You make it sound simple."

"It won't be. Nothing about this job has been simple, but the rewards will more than make up for our hard work."

Haakon once again found himself at the Blood safe house having failed to claim the seal to the demon prison. This was why he hated fighting wizards. They had so many different ways to flee. And none of them were hesitant to use them when they saw him coming. They might be cowards, but they were smart cowards.

The real problem was his hound getting destroyed. And it wasn't Cristo that did it. That young man in the black t-shirt blew his spell away like it was nothing. And while the hound wasn't nearly as powerful as his armor, it was a fairly high-level spell. It would take more than a simple, weak dispel magic spell to end it.

He sat on the too-narrow bed, pulled out his phone, and hit redial.

"Since you're calling me from the safe house and not our private plane, I assume you failed," Lord Solomon said.

"The thieves fled rather than face me."

"Of course they did. We didn't hire them because they were stupid. Pity we didn't realize they were disloyal. It wasn't their reputation. How do you plan to proceed?"

"My hound was destroyed. I thought I'd rest until morning and summon it again. Perhaps if I can take them by surprise, I'll have better luck."

"You'd best hope you do."

Before Lord Solomon could hang up Haakon said, "A question, if I may, my lord?"

"Go ahead."

"Another wizard interfered with my mission. He looked like a Kugo but didn't use fire magic."

"Daisuke. I should've known the Circle would send him. That young man is exceedingly dangerous. Do not underestimate him if you value your life."

"What sort of magic does he use?"

"That's what makes him so dangerous. While he's primarily a necromancer, he's studied many sorts of magic and is competent in all of them. Ironically, the only sort of magic he's poor at is spirit magic."

Haakon hesitated before asking, "How do you know so much about him, my lord?"

"I tried to recruit him. He's one of us, Haakon, though he refuses to accept his proper place."

Haakon's blue eyes got very wide indeed. "He's of the blood yet refused your call to battle? How foolish."

"Indeed, but Daisuke's lack of vision isn't your concern.

Get the seal and bring it back along with the prison. Should anyone get in your way, kill them. Clear?"

"Yes, my lord. No matter how many tries it takes, I will claim the seal for the Blood of Solomon."

The line went dead and Haakon grimaced. If the youth was of the blood, that explained his gift for magic. It also meant he was a far more dangerous opponent than Haakon had first imagined.

He took Erik's Helm off and set it on the stand beside his bed. No matter how strong he was, there was no one that could defeat Haakon while he wore the artifact.

No matter what it took, he swore that he'd get the seal and lay it, along with the prison, at his lord's feet.

CHAPTER FOURTEEN

Natsumi drove at a much more reasonable speed back toward the estate. That suited Daisuke, as, having survived an encounter with Haakon, dying in a car crash didn't appeal to him. Even better, she hadn't felt the need to pester him with questions. Given how few answers he had, it would've been a waste of time for both of them.

You're unlikely to die in a car crash, Master, given your magical protections.

You might be right, but I'm not eager to test the theory.

His phone rang. "Boss?"

"We lost them, Daisuke. Haakon drove northwest out of the city. Wherever he went, there are no cameras. We never reestablished contact with Cristo and Itsuko. Given that they've changed cars, I'm not sure how we'll find them again."

"I'm sure you'll manage, boss. Natsumi told the cops to keep their eyes open but not to approach no matter what. I got some of Itsuko's blood and we're headed to the Kugo estate so I can whip up a tracking spell of my own."

"Good work. As long as Cristo doesn't ditch her somewhere, you should have no trouble finding them."

"He won't ditch her. When she was wounded I finally figured out something. Itsuko isn't just muscle that acts as his bodyguard. She's his familiar. Taking her out might make an opening to get a kill shot on him."

"A human familiar, that's rare outside of vampires. Since there's nothing else I can do at the moment, I'll wish you luck."

"Thanks, boss. Make sure you get some rest. You sound all in."

She chuckled. "You sound more like my father than my subordinate sometimes."

"Goodnight, boss." He hung up and pocketed his phone.

"You two sound close."

His gaze shifted to Natsumi. "She works really hard and sometimes forgets to take care of herself. In addition to field work, I'm also a part-time nursemaid, at least it feels that way. Since the Circle wouldn't run nearly as efficiently if she got sick and couldn't work, keeping her healthy is a good thing for everyone."

"You're not fooling me. I heard the concern in your voice. Are you two a couple?"

Daisuke barked a laugh. "Hardly. She's hot enough, but doesn't exactly give off an 'I'm interested' vibe. Besides, hooking up with the boss isn't a good idea in any organization, much less one that does what we do."

"I can't argue with that. What did you mean when you said Itsuko was Cristo's familiar?"

He cocked his head. "What do you mean, what do I mean?"

"I thought humans took spirits or demons or some other kind of magical creature as familiars. I've never heard of one human taking another as a familiar."

"I'm not surprised you haven't heard of it. It's fairly common among the vampire clans, but other than that, exceedingly rare. Basically, as long as both parties are willing, anyone can become the familiar of a wizard. It creates a spiritual link that allows you to share your thoughts and feelings. It also makes sharing spells more efficient. As the wizard, Cristo is dominant. Essentially he can compel Itsuko to do whatever he wants. On the downside, if I were to kill Itsuko, the psychic backlash would hurt and weaken Cristo, though he'd recover in a month or two."

"Sounds risky for him but why would she agree to such an arrangement?"

Daisuke shrugged. "You'd have to ask her. Maybe they're in love."

She glanced his way, one eyebrow perfectly arched in disbelief.

"Okay, probably not. It's not like her reasons matter anyway. We still need to deal with them."

"About that. Does your group have a prison or something for the enemies they defeat?"

"No."

"I see. Then... never mind."

They reached the dirt road that led to the estate and turned down it. Both guards waved them through without issue. Surprising given what had just happened. Daisuke had expected them to be even more alert than last time he visited. Maybe they figured anyone visiting either had a reason or would kill them if they interfered. Not a great attitude for a guard.

Natsumi pulled into the garage and as soon as he got out,

Daisuke turned for the mansion. Given how little had changed, he assumed the workshop would be in the same spot.

"Where are you going?"

"I told you, I need to use the workshop."

"You need to talk to your mother first."

"Tell her where I am. I can talk while I make preparations." So saying he set out again.

A few servants glanced at him as he passed, but no one spoke. They probably didn't know what to say to the ghost wandering their halls. Since he had no idea what to say to them, Daisuke kept his mouth shut and kept walking.

When he reached the workshop he slid the door open and stepped inside. Finally, a room that had been updated. All the latest alchemy equipment was lined up in neat rows on shelves around the room. Containers of reagents, precious metals, and gems covered other shelves while two workbenches dominated the center of the room. Everything he needed and then some.

Ruq, now a rat again, climbed up on the table. "That girl called me a creature."

"You are a creature." Daisuke selected a vial and transferred Itsuko's blood from its ethereal bubble to the glass cylinder. That went into a holder and onto the empty workbench.

"True, but it's rude to say it out loud like that. What if she hurt my feelings?"

"I'm confident your feelings can handle a good deal more than that." Daisuke collected a silver rod along with some powdered crystal, a slate, and chalk. Those joined the blood on his workbench.

"Daisuke." He glanced at the door and found his mother just outside.

"Hi, Mom. What did you need?"

"I wanted to talk to you."

"Sure, go ahead. It's going to take me at least fifteen minutes to make all the preparations I need."

"Could we go somewhere and sit?" She looked quickly at Ruq then away. "Just the two of us."

"Ruq's my familiar." The imp waved but said nothing. "Anything you tell me, he'll instantly know. Anyway, I really need to get this done. There are some bad people out there that need stopping. The longer I delay, the better the odds that something awful happens."

She stepped inside and closed the door behind her. "It's about your father."

Daisuke perked up at that. "Did you remember something?"

"I meant Yoshikazu."

"Oh." Daisuke started drawing a magic circle large enough to surround the silver rod on the slate. "What about him?"

"Though he couldn't say anything publicly, he really did hope to put the bad blood between you aside."

The chalk fell silent and he looked up. "Did you really send Natsumi to bring me here just to tell me that?"

She winced as if Daisuke had slapped her and he immediately regretted his tone if not his words. "He took a lot of damage in the fight. Sako still isn't sure if he's going to survive. I thought maybe you could tell him you forgive him, just in case the worst happens."

"That's all? Sure, I'll pop in when I'm finished."

"Have you forgiven him?"

Daisuke resumed drawing. "In the sense that I no longer dream about murdering him, yes. Beyond that, I couldn't care less what happens to him one way or the other. You and

Shogo are the only members of the clan that mean anything to me. Well, Natsumi's growing on me a little. But other than you three, I wouldn't lose a night's sleep if the entire clan dropped dead tomorrow."

He stopped again and looked up. "What I can't figure out is why, by all the archangels in heaven, you care about the clan. You were forced to marry into the Kugo clan. They kicked me out and kept you from contacting me, yet you still seem to care about them. About him. And please, I beg you, don't tell me it's complicated."

His mother said nothing. Whether she couldn't or didn't want to explain her feelings, he didn't know. Daisuke wanted to understand where she was coming from, but couldn't. Maybe he never would.

He finished the circle and placed the silver rod in the center.

"If there's nothing else, I need to start casting."

"Of course. I'll be waiting at the healer's office. Please stop by before you leave."

"Will do."

"I love you, sweetheart."

He looked up, smiled, and said, "Love you too."

Despite his barely suppressed rage at the clan, he knew deep down his mother hadn't been to blame. She was as helpless before the stupid clan traditions as he had been.

His mother slipped out and silently closed the door behind her.

Putting her out of his mind, Daisuke gathered the ether and started forming the seeking spell. Let's see the bastards hide once he was finished.

After parting ways with Daisuke at the garage, Natsumi made her way to the healer's office. The yard had been cleaned up and, save for a few scorch marks, there was no sign of the previous night's battle. The bodies had probably been reduced to ash, the souls of the dead having gone to join the spirits. An official report would have to be made, but that would keep until Uncle Yoshikazu was better.

The door was closed when she arrived, but there was no sign indicating treatment was underway. She knocked then slid it open. Most of the injured had been moved, probably back to their rooms where immediate family would look after them. Only her father and uncle remained. Shogo sat in one of the few chairs, awake but with drooping eyelids. He still wore his hastily donned, rumpled clothes. She seriously doubted he'd gotten a wink of sleep since the fight.

"You okay?"

He looked up at her and yawned. "Under the circumstances, I guess so. You?"

"Same. Where's Aunt Kiyoko? I brought Daisuke."

"I know. We saw him headed for the house, so Mom went to talk to him." Shogo sat up in his chair. "Does he hate us?"

Natsumi grabbed a chair for herself and sat with a long sigh. "I don't think he hates you or your mother. He saved my life twice, so I'm pretty sure he doesn't hate me either."

"What about the rest of the clan?"

Natsumi shrugged. "I'm less optimistic there. How are they?"

"Sako was here about an hour ago and said they were stable. Her magic is doing its best, but healing's going to take days if not weeks."

His response didn't surprise her. "Stable is good at least. If you want to hit the sack, I can stay here until your mom gets back."

Shogo shook his head. "I want to talk to Daisuke. I'm the only one that hasn't had a chance yet."

She nodded, in no way inclined to discourage him. A quick look at her father confirmed that he at least hadn't gotten worse. Getting his arm regenerated would be the most important thing once he woke up. Even Sako's magic couldn't manage that. She wasn't sure whose could, but Natsumi vowed to herself that she'd find out.

The door opened again and Aunt Kiyoko stepped in. Somehow, despite everything that had happened, she looked as elegant as always in her red kimono. Her eyes told another story; they were dark and bloodshot. Had she been crying?

"Did that idiot say something to upset you?" Natsumi asked.

"Nothing I didn't already suspect. He did agree to stop here before he left, which is more than I'd hoped for to be honest."

Natsumi stood. "I'll give him a piece of my mind."

Aunt Kiyoko put a gentle hand on her arm. "Not now. He's in the middle of some magical ritual."

"I guess he does still hate us," Shogo said, sounding even more depressed.

"I'll beat some sense into him." She still had Flame Edge. She might not be a match for that blond monster, but her cousin was another matter. It was time someone made it clear to him that family obligations didn't go away just because you were in a bad mood.

Half an hour later there was a knock and the door slid open. Daisuke looked at each of them in turn. He had a silver rod in his hand and it glowed in the ether. It had to be the seeking device he talked about.

He grinned and nodded to Shogo. "Good to see you, little brother."

Shogo smiled back, seeming a little relieved.

Next he went to his father and whispered something she didn't catch before turning to his mother. "Good enough?"

Aunt Kiyoko nodded. "Thank you, dear."

"Okay, I'm leaving to hunt down a pair of murderous thieves." He looked at Natsumi. "You coming or staying?"

"Oh, I'm coming, but first we need to settle something. Let's step outside. I don't want to bother our fathers."

"Why does everyone want to sort things out in the middle of a crisis? This won't keep until later?"

"No."

She stalked past him and out into the yard. When she was a safe distance from the healer's office she spun around and put a hand on Flame Edge's hilt. Daisuke stood a few paces away and Shogo and Aunt Kiyoko were watching from the walkway.

"Whatever you've got to say, spit it out. I'm in a hurry."

She ground her teeth then forced herself to relax. "You need to apologize for the way you've been acting. Whatever you might think about the clan, it's still your family and you have a responsibility to help out in a time of crisis."

He stared at her for a second then threw his head back and laughed.

Her temper, which she'd barely been keeping under control since Aunt Kiyoko came back with tears in her eyes, exploded. She drew Flame Edge and crimson fire ran down its length.

"If you refuse, we'll settle it with a match, just like we used to."

His eyes went cold and hard. The laughter drained from his face and a chill ran down her spine. Even during the earlier battles, she'd never seen him with this expression.

"If you draw a sword on me, Princess, you'd better be ready to use it."

She swallowed hard but refused to back down. "So you want to settle it in a match?"

"A match?" His lip quirked up. "You against me isn't a match, it's a slaughter."

"Stop this, both of you!" Aunt Kiyoko shouted.

Daisuke ignored her, his gaze never wavering.

She'd show him how much stronger she'd gotten since he left.

Natsumi gathered herself to charge.

Daisuke's eyes turned bloodred and where the irises had been black lines appeared, forming a pentagram.

The flames vanished from her sword and a fire spirit that looked like a red-furred kitten fell to the ground. It writhed around as if in pain, steam rising off its body. It was the fire spirit bound to Flame Edge.

She stared at Daisuke. "You're killing her."

"You'll find it considerably harder to win the match without the spirit's power backing you up." His voice was as cold as the winter snow. "This is the magic I spent three years mastering: anti-spirit magic. I dreamed of coming back here and showing it to all of you that cast me out. To show you just how pathetic your precious spirit magic was. At least I dreamed of it until I found a better path."

He blinked and his eyes were back to normal. The fire kitten shook all over, hopped to her feet, and leapt into the blade.

"I'm calling this my win, unless you wish to continue."

Natsumi sheathed Flame Edge. It took all of her self-control not to tremble. Was he really that strong or was she just that weak? "I don't."

"Good. That's the smartest thing you've said since I got

back. I'm borrowing your car." He threw a wave over his shoulder. "Mom, Shogo, so long."

"Like hell you're borrowing my car. I'm coming with you."

He shrugged, but didn't slow. She hurried to catch up with him, uncertain what to say after what just happened. The silence lingered as they pulled out of the garage and headed back to the main road.

As she turned onto the asphalt Natsumi finally said, "I've never heard of anti-spirit magic."

"I'm not surprised." He pointed the silver rod until it glowed. Looked like they were still in the city. "Given that spirit magic is just about the only form of magic officially sanctioned in Japan, teaching people how best to defeat spirits makes little sense. Out in the wider world, that prohibition doesn't exist. And even if it did, the people I learned from wouldn't have cared."

"You'd think someone would've said something about it, even if only so spirit magic users would be ready to defend against it."

"I don't know what to tell you. I certainly don't make the rules here. Assuming he ever wakes up, you can ask Yoshikazu."

His indifferent tone got her back up again, but she immediately dismissed the emotion. "Do you know, I haven't heard you call Uncle Yoshikazu Dad since you got here."

"That right?"

"Why?"

Daisuke frowned and she feared he might get angry again. But the moment passed and instead he said, "If I tell you why, do you promise not to mention the clan again?"

"Promise."

He told her about the DNA test and his mother's one-night stand. Natsumi had trouble processing the story. It didn't mesh at all with what she knew about Aunt Kiyoko. Of course, people could change a lot in twenty-three years.

"That's... something," she said when he fell silent.

"Yeah, that's one word for it. So now you know why I failed my initiation. Feel free to tell anyone you like. Should you mention it to Yoshikazu, get a picture of his face and text it to me. I promised Mom I'd keep it to myself, but it was the only way I could think of to shut you up."

Natsumi shook her head. Understanding his bitterness did nothing to make it more pleasant.

"You need to make the next left. We're getting close."

And just like that he was all business again. Much as she'd wanted to know him better, all business wasn't such a bad thing right now.

CHAPTER FIFTEEN

Cristo's first choice for a hideout wouldn't have been a by-the-hour love hotel, but desperate times and all that. At the very least the bored clerk that checked them in hadn't given him and Itsuko more than a passing glance. Given the reaction of the police earlier, he had to assume that they were wanted and that their names and descriptions had been plastered everywhere in the city. The young man's indifference may have saved his life.

Their room was surprisingly well furnished, with a table and chairs to go with the heart-shaped bed. Itsuko was sound asleep on the bed. Even though he'd healed her with magic and stolen life force, getting shot still took a lot out of a person. For his part, Cristo had used a portion of the life energy to wash away his weariness. He wanted to do a bit of testing before seeking out Haakon tonight.

The demon seal sat on the table in front of him. A thin disk of bronze engraved with a unique rune, it didn't really look like much; even in the ether it gave off only a faint glow. If you didn't know what it was, no one would even consider it valuable as anything more than a curiosity. He had to give Solomon the Wise credit; making something of great worth look worthless was a fine way to keep it safe.

Gathering ether into the tip of his finger, Cristo touched the edge of the seal. He created a resonance connection and immediately felt himself pulled north and west. Good, it connected to the prison with no issues. He'd feared Haakon might've created a ward to block seeking magic. Given how powerful he was, Haakon probably didn't fear anyone showing up to try and steal it.

It could also be a trap.

A quick spiritual scouting trip wouldn't be a guarantee that he'd find any potential dangers, but it was still worth the effort. Cristo closed his eyes.

Before he could activate the spell that would free his spirit from his body, the alarm he'd set outside the hotel triggered. He'd set it to activate if either the Kugo brats or Haakon showed up.

He shifted the focus of his spell and soon found himself staring at the hotel entrance. He caught a glimpse of a slender man in a black t-shirt just before the door closed. The Kugo pair then. Better than Haakon at least.

The seal went into his pocket and Cristo shook Itsuko awake.

Her eyes popped open, instantly on alert. "What is it?"

"Our enemies have proven more tenacious than I hoped."

"Haakon?" Itsuko rolled out of bed and started pulling on her shoes.

"No, the other two."

"How the hell did they find us?"

"An excellent question. The only answer I can come up with is your wound. When the bullet passed through, it would've taken some blood with it. Certainly enough to make a viable tracing spell."

She stood, ready to go. "What's the plan?"

"I fear we're going to have to split up. You can lead our hunters on a merry chase while I try and collect the prison."

"I don't like it."

"Nor do I, but our options are limited." Cristo gathered ether and opened another dimensional door. They emerged in a parking lot half a mile from the hotel where they'd left the van. "I'll contact you when I have the prison. Good luck."

He jogged off before she could offer any more arguments. Going up against Haakon alone was indeed madness, but it was his only option now and he'd make it work or die trying.

"Ugh, are you sure this is the right place?" The look on Natsumi's face when she pulled into the love hotel's parking lot did wonders to dispel Daisuke's bad mood. He packed his conflicting emotions away. He had work to do and he couldn't let them get in the way.

It was about as tacky a place as he'd ever seen and given how much of Europe Daisuke had traveled, that was saying something. There were flashing neon hearts above a sign that advertised rooms by the hour, free bedside condoms, and no extra charge for XXX movies.

Class all the way, no doubt about it.

He pointed the silver rod at the hotel and it lit up like a flashlight. "This is it. Do you have some kind of official ID so we can get the clerk to let us in?"

She grabbed Flame Edge. "I can let us in."

"I take that as a no."

They got out and Daisuke opened the front door. As it

closed behind him he made a mental note to find some hand sanitizer as soon as possible.

That's hardly the most disgusting thing you've ever touched.

I'll thank you to keep the comments on my ex-girlfriends to a minimum.

He'd left Ruq outside to watch in case the thieves tried to sneak out. They hoped to take the pair by surprise, but when magic was involved, that was harder than it sounded.

A skinny, pimple-faced guy behind the counter looked up as they approached. His eyes nearly bugged out of his head. Whether it was because of Natsumi's looks or her sword, Daisuke wasn't certain.

He was about to speak when the light on the tracker dimmed.

"Shit! They're gone."

"What!" Natsumi glared at him as if it was his fault. She'd been pretty quiet since their showdown and he found he was glad to see her getting back to normal. He'd lost his cool worse than he intended back at the estate. Though nowhere near as bad as it used to be, the old anger had been running much closer to the surface since he reached Japan.

"He must've set an alarm spell. I didn't see anything, but there are plenty of ways to hide such a thing. Come on, let's get after them before they put any more distance between us."

"The sooner we get out of here the better."

They retreated to the car, leaving the still-gaping clerk staring at their backs. He'd have a story to tell his buddies at the bar tonight.

"Where to?" Natsumi asked.

Daisuke pointed the silver rod and it was brightest on the opposite side of the hotel.

Natsumi pulled around and drove through a stop sign

before taking a left. The rod grew quickly brighter before dimming again.

"They've got to be in a car. I wish I knew what they were driving."

Natsumi stepped on it and said, "Just point that thing at everyone we pass. We'll find them sooner or later."

The light dimmed again and a quick swing left and right confirmed that they'd made a turn to the left. Natsumi made the next left, but judging by the tracker, they were one street too late.

"This is ridiculous," she said. "We're never going to catch up to them at this rate."

Daisuke glanced at her. "If you have another idea, I'm all ears."

"I don't and it's pissing me off."

He knew how she felt, but there wasn't any other way to do this. Eventually Cristo and Itsuko would run out of gas. As long as they did so before he and Natsumi did, they'd catch up eventually.

His phone rang and he offered a silent prayer that the boss had good news.

"Yeah, boss."

"We caught Cristo on a traffic cam headed north. Based on Crystal's calculations, he's moving toward Haakon."

They were chasing the pair southeast. How could Cristo be on his way north?

"Shit! They split up. Itsuko is leading us away from her partner. Five'll get you ten he's planning a one-on-one fight with Haakon."

"That's insane," the boss said. "They aren't a match for him together, much less one-on-one."

"Maybe, maybe not. Cristo might be able to wear him

down if he has a flight spell active and long-range attacks. That's how I'd fight Haakon if I had to."

"What's going on?" Natsumi asked.

"Looks like the thieves split up. Cristo's on his way north to fight Haakon. At least that's my guess."

"So do we keep after Itsuko or turn north to join the fight with Cristo?"

"Turn north; Itsuko's irrelevant. Boss, can you have Crystal keep an eye out for Itsuko? She's going to need gas at some point and you might get lucky again. The cops can probably take her as long as she's on her own."

"We'll do our best. Be careful, Daisuke."

Careful had ceased to be an option days ago.

He tucked his phone away and held on for dear life as Natsumi did a one-eighty in the middle of a busy street before flooring it again. If the wizard thing didn't work out, she'd have a great future in drift racing.

CHAPTER SIXTEEN

Haakon lay on his too-small bed and stared at the ceiling. There was nothing to do until he could summon the hound again, and he was bored. Television didn't interest him. He spoke no Japanese and translation spells were outside his area of expertise. He could've trained, but didn't want to waste his magic when on a mission lest he find himself short.

So he lay still and stared at nothing in particular while his mind wandered. He kept Erik's Helm at his side and the demon prison in his pocket. Neither artifact was ever more than an arm's length from him. From the time he'd begun training as a warrior it had been drilled into him that you never left yourself unarmed when in enemy territory. And while he might not actually be at war with Japan, Haakon considered anywhere outside the Blood of Solomon's head-quarters to be enemy territory.

That philosophy had saved him on several occasions.

His hand was halfway to the TV remote when the front of the safe house exploded inward.

Scrambling to his feet, he plunked Erik's Helm on his head and sent ether into it. The magical armor appeared around him and the golden ax formed in his hand. Ready for anything, he strode out into the yard.

Cristo hovered twenty feet in the air directly in front of him. Black wings had sprouted from the man's back and dark energy gathered around both his hands. All in all he looked a good deal more impressive than he had during their previous encounter.

Not that it would matter as long as he had his armor.

Never one to mince words, Haakon threw his ax with all his might.

Cristo dodged it easily and countered with a blast that skipped off Haakon's armor.

A new ax appeared in his hand.

"Give me the seal and you can live," Haakon said. "You'll get no better offer."

"Since I'm up here and you're down there, I hardly think you're in any position to make threats. Your armor will run out of power eventually and when it does, my magic will rip you to pieces."

Shining golden wings sprang out of Haakon's back.

A single lash sent him rocketing into the air, right at Cristo.

The traitor dodged Haakon's ax with inches to spare.

He banked right and dove at Cristo again.

Using the armor's flight ability took a lot more power and vastly shortened how long Haakon could maintain the magic.

His ax struck a barrier and sent Cristo tumbling across the sky.

Haakon kept after him, not bothering to dodge the occasional weak spell that came his way.

They clashed again and again.

Somehow Cristo managed to stay just enough out of his way to survive. But that couldn't last.

With a great mental effort, Haakon pushed himself even faster.

His golden ax landed a square blow and sent Cristo crashing into the ground hard enough to dent the earth.

Haakon quickly landed and dismissed his wings. He only had a couple minutes left and the authorities would no doubt be here soon. He didn't want to face dozens of armed men without his armor.

Best to collect the seal and hurry back to the airport.

He stalked over, wary of any potential trap. Such caution proved unnecessary. Cristo lay unmoving in a divot a foot deep. He'd put up a better fight than Haakon had expected. Enemy or not, he respected anyone with that sort of strength.

Taking a knee beside the body, Haakon started patting him down.

He'd barely gotten started when a burst of black lightning sent him sprawling.

Figuring out exactly where Haakon and Cristo were turned out to be way easier than Daisuke had feared it might be. Between the tremors running through the ether and the two figures battling in the sky, their location was pretty obvious.

Natsumi was staring at the aerial duel and paying not nearly enough attention to the road. "Did you know he could fly?"

"Which one?"

"Either of them."

"Flight is a fairly simple spell, but it takes a lot of power to maintain for extended periods. It looks to me like Cristo did a partial demon summoning and is using its power for himself. Which makes a lot of sense given his specialty. I shudder to think what price he had to pay the demon, but that's not my problem. As for Haakon, no, I had no idea he could fly. None of our intel indicates that the armor could do that. But to be fair, all we know about it is what's been observed in the field, so he probably never had to use it before."

She whipped down a side road and they roared past a couple cottages. The residents were staring at the airborne battle with slack-jawed expressions. He didn't blame them. Though he might be better at hiding it, Daisuke felt pretty much the same way. He debated getting his staff out of storage, but dismissed the idea. He didn't have time and the power boost wouldn't be enough to make a huge difference against Haakon.

Natsumi stopped in the middle of the road directly across from the battle and they got out. The nearest cottage had a massive hole blown in it. As they sprinted forward, he paused long enough to blast the tires of a two-door parked in the driveway. If Haakon wanted to get away this time, he could walk.

They came around the cottage just in time to see Cristo slam into the ground with spine-shattering force. The impact blasted his wings away and he wasn't moving. Daisuke could still see a little bit of life in him, but not much.

Haakon landed and knelt beside Cristo, seeming intent on dealing with what little life remained and claiming the seal. Daisuke didn't especially care if he finished Cristo off, but no way could he be allowed to claim the seal.

Daisuke hurled a bolt of black lightning that sent Haakon stumbling back. That told him a great deal about how much power Haakon had left.

Damn little.

This might be the best chance they'd ever have to finish Haakon off.

"Murderer!" Natsumi drew Flame Edge and charged.

She slashed and dodged an ax strike.

Her sword still couldn't get through Haakon's armor.

She screamed and kept slicing. Unfortunately, she was right between him and Haakon, which severely restricted the spells he could use.

Haakon surged forward, hitting her with a shoulder tackle that sent Natsumi flying.

When he did, his armor flickered.

This was Daisuke's chance.

He summoned a black disk under Haakon's feet and black lightning crackled out of it.

The armor survived the first two hits then it shattered.

Haakon howled in pain as the blasts burned away his life force inch by inch.

A new lance of black energy shot in, shredding Haakon's pants and sending the prison tumbling to the ground. As soon as it hit, the lance transformed into a claw that grabbed the prison and dragged it back to Cristo.

Before Daisuke could react, Cristo fell into a doorway and vanished.

"Damn it!"

He turned his full fury on Haakon. The giant Norseman somehow pulled a thin wooden rod out of his undamaged pocket and snapped it. The moment he did, he vanished.

"Damn it!"

Daisuke ended his spell and hurried over to Natsumi's

limp form. There was no blood, so he assumed she just had the wind knocked out of her.

He gave her a shake. "Hey. If you're alive, say something."

She groaned. "I'm alive. I hurt too much for it to be otherwise. Did you get him?"

"No. Cristo was playing opossum. While I was dealing with Haakon, he stole the prison. Now he's got both pieces and we have no idea where he might have gone."

"Is that as bad as it sounds?"

"It's worse."

Cristo had never been in as much pain as he was right now. Not only did his body hurt from the tip of his toes to the top of his head, but opening that last dimensional door had left him with a screaming backlash headache. If a five-year-old with a stick showed up right now looking for trouble, he'd have no hope of winning the fight.

On the plus side, the pain meant that Haakon's last blow hadn't broken his spine. A small comfort, but right now he'd take what he could get. Especially since he should be dead. Only the timely arrival of a different set of enemies had saved him.

He sighed, tried to sit up, and failed. Alright, where had he ended up? Usually he cast the spell with a specific destination in mind, but this time he'd simply thought of the most distant, safe location the spell could reach. He was lying on grass and there were no buildings visible. That likely put him in some farmer's pasture. He'd passed quite a few small farms on his way to Haakon's cabin, so that made sense.

Closing his eyes, he focused on his link with Itsuko. It was still strong, good. Calling her to him was a risk assuming his enemies were still able to track her, but he was too weak to do anything else. Summoning the demon in his current condition was madness. He'd have no hope of focusing his will enough to compel its obedience even with the seal.

Itsuko.

No response. The link was still there, which meant she was alive. She must be far enough away that his psychic voice wasn't reaching her.

He took a deep breath and steadied himself.

ITSUKO!

Where are you? What's going on? I haven't seen any sign of pursuit and I'm getting low on gas.

He'd reached her, thank heaven for that.

Calm down. I got the prison, but Haakon left me in rough shape. I need you to come pick me up. Follow the psychic link.

How? I don't know anything about that magic stuff.

I'll make the connection as strong as I can. If you concentrate, you'll be able to tell where I am. Get here as quickly as you can. I'm sure the Kugo pair are looking for me as we speak.

I'm on my way.

Her thoughts didn't indicate confidence. Well, confident or not, she was his only hope of getting out of here alive.

Cristo ran his thumb across the smooth bronze of the prison. He had to survive. Dying when he was so close to ultimate victory would be cruel beyond words.

And while he knew that cruelty was part of the universe's very nature, he refused to believe all his years of effort would come to nothing.

Focusing beyond the pain, Cristo sent his will through the link to Itsuko. Encouragement mingled with desperation to hopefully spur her to haste. But not too much. Getting pulled over by a cop would be ruinous right now.

Time meant nothing to him as he focused every fiber of

his being on his connection to Itsuko. It grew slowly closer, minute by agonizing minute until finally... "You look like hell."

He opened his eyes and looked up at Itsuko. "I feel considerably worse than that. Did you have any trouble?"

"I passed a bunch of cops on my way. They were all parked by a cabin that looked like a bomb went off in front of it. I assume that's where you had your fight."

"A safe assumption. Help me up. We need to get out of here before our hunters arrive."

She grabbed his hand and pulled him to his feet before slinging his arm around her shoulders. Cristo leaned heavily on her and somehow shuffled his feet enough to make slow progress toward where he assumed the van waited.

"Just so you know, I'm down to about a gallon of gas, so we're not getting far."

"You just need to get me somewhere safe to rest, then you need to head out again."

"I can't leave you alone in this shape."

"Assuming the Kugo brats still have a way to track you, staying with me will be the greater risk. Once I can use my magic again, I'll open the prison and free the demon within. When I have control over it, the hunters will become the prey."

CHAPTER SEVENTEEN

While Natsumi was busy explaining to the many police officers that had arrived after a number of calls to emergency services, Daisuke went a little ways off and reported in. The boss hadn't been thrilled with his news. Daisuke wasn't thrilled with it either, but he'd done the best he could all things considered.

The only good news to come out of the whole mess was that Haakon was now off the board. The stick he broke probably held a stored teleportation spell. With any luck he was halfway around the world at whatever passed for the Blood of Solomon's base. Maybe Daisuke would get lucky and Solomon the Great would finish what he started.

His lip curled in a humorless smile. And maybe pigs would fly. No one would be stupid enough to discard someone as powerful as Haakon lightly. No, he feared the giant Norseman would continue to be a problem for the foreseeable future.

But not here and not now.

He took the seeking rod out and turned a slow circle. It

quickly lit up and got steadily brighter. Itsuko was headed this way, almost certainly to pick up Cristo.

Natsumi was still deep in conversation with a pair of cops. They didn't have time to waste. "Ruq, you're up."

What do you wish me to do?

Take to the air. I'll see if I can guide you to Itsuko. If you can at least see what kind of car she's driving, it'll make them easier to track.

On my way.

Ruq leapt into the sky, once more in raven form. With their minds linked, Daisuke could see through his familiar's eyes and Ruq knew roughly which direction the seeker was pointing.

The line kept shifting and soon they were flying over small pastures that dotted the area. A few fat cows munched on grass, but no people were visible. The commotion probably convinced them to stay inside. Just as well as he doubted Itsuko would hesitate to kill anyone that caused her trouble.

A few seconds later he spotted a pair of figures struggling across one of the fields.

That's them.

Ruq started circling the pair. Just off the field waited a tan van. Ruq's powerful vision allowed him to make out the license plate. Daisuke made a note of it to tell the boss.

Itsuko loaded Cristo into the back of the van and took off. Ruq followed as long as he could, but eventually had to circle back. Their link extended only so far and he'd reached the edge of it, damn the luck.

At least they had a direction now.

Come on back. Looks like Natsumi's about done with the cops.

Daisuke loosened his connection with Ruq and took a moment to get used to being totally in his own body again. The transition from flying to standing always left him dizzy for a second. A couple blinks got him straightened out and not a moment too soon.

Natsumi was headed his way.

"We good?" he asked.

"Yeah, I had to prove my credentials. For some reason this precinct didn't have me in the database. They claimed technical issues. Anyway, where do we stand?"

He filled her in on what he'd learned. He pointed up the road. "They were headed that way in a tan van. I suggest we get after them. I'd like to finish this before Cristo recovers enough to free the demon."

"I second that." They climbed into her car and Natsumi took off up the road. "So what's the worst-case scenario if Cristo frees this demon?"

Daisuke told her what the boss told him about the giant hurricane. "The problem, and I seriously doubt Cristo knows this, is that if he doesn't know the demon's true name, even having the seal won't be enough to fully control it. He should be able to protect himself, but the demon is likely to go on a rampage."

"Do you know his true name?"

"Yeah, the boss looked it up in the Book of Wisdom. He's called Vorgon, an elder demon in service to Narukami Tempest. He was the most powerful of the nine he sent against Solomon the Wise."

Daisuke checked the seeker. She was still somewhere ahead of them.

"If you can't control the demon without knowing that, why would anyone bother trying to claim the prison?"

"The names are recorded in places beside the Book of Wisdom. Worshippers of Narukami Tempest could ask their master. There are a number of apocalyptic death cults that would be happy to set the demon free just to watch it destroy

Japan. As far as Cristo is concerned, I suspect he's just ignorant of all the necessary steps. Even in magic circles, that's pretty esoteric knowledge."

Itsuko made a sharp right ahead of them somewhere.

"Slow down and keep an eye out for anywhere she might have let Cristo off." Daisuke got his phone out and called the boss. "Looks like they split up again."

"Are you sure?"

"I'm not sure of anything, but if we chase her and they're not together, we'll be getting farther away all the time."

"Alright, we'll keep watch for the van and keep you posted."

"Thanks, boss." He disconnected.

Natsumi inched along until they reached a rough, rutted dirt driveway. It was long enough that he couldn't see any building at the end. Seemed like a good place to hide out.

"Let's check down there."

She obliged him, turning up the driveway and easing through the ruts slowly enough that none of his organs shifted. It was reassuring to know that she could drive like a sane person when necessary.

The driveway ended in an open circle of dirt. A small house sat directly ahead of them and a much larger barn loomed to the right. The barn's door was open. That didn't prove anything, but it did make him curious.

"I'll check the barn, you check the house. If you have any sort of official ID, this would be a good time to show it."

"All I have is the car tag and my license. Don't worry, everyone knows the Kugo name. That'll be enough to get us any cooperation we need."

Daisuke nodded and got out of the car. He hoped she was right. Not that he really expected any trouble out here. Guns were rare and wizards rarer. If he was being honest, neither posed much of a threat to him unless they were especially powerful.

Just to be safe he conjured an extra layer of magical protection.

What about me?

"Get up on the barn roof. I doubt Cristo is in any shape to run, but just to be safe I want you on lookout."

He sensed his invisible familiar fly into position. Satisfied that he was as ready as he could be, Daisuke stepped into the barn. The stink of animals and manure assaulted his nose. And people wondered why he didn't like country life.

Daisuke tiptoed down the central aisle, checking each stall as he went. Each one held hay and nothing else. He sensed no one hiding. A single life force would be easy to spot in the empty barn. It looked like his theory about the pair splitting up had been off the mark.

Outside the barn he took a deep breath of fresh air. No word from the boss yet. If Itsuko avoided the city, spotting her would be a lot harder. Ruq landed on the roof of the car and transformed from a raven to his favored rat form. Daisuke absently stroked Ruq's head as he thought.

Itsuko couldn't take him to a hospital, that would be a sure way of getting caught. The best modern medicine could do for Cristo in the short term was numb the pain and Daisuke seriously doubted that the warlock would want to risk losing control for any length of time.

He checked the tracker and found the glow alarmingly dim. Itsuko had put plenty of miles between her and them. All because of his wrong guess.

Daisuke wanted to blow something up, but lacked any suitable targets.

Natsumi finally emerged from the house and hurried to join him.

"I take it you found someone to talk to?"

"Yes. Even better, the farmer's wife saw the van. It pulled in, sat in the driveway for a couple minutes, turned around, and pulled back out. No one got out. She assumed they were lost." They got in the car and Natsumi asked, "What now?"

"We resume the chase. If they stopped here, Cristo must have intended to get out and hide. If he didn't, something must have happened. Maybe we'll get lucky and his injuries will finish him off."

"If Cristo's dead, can Itsuko open the prison?" Natsumi turned around and headed for the main road.

"Sure, all she needs to do is put the seal in place. But she has no magical ability and thus no hope of controlling Vorgon. She has to know that."

"Why?"

He stared, uncertain what she was getting at. "What do you mean, why?"

"Why do you assume she would know that? If Cristo didn't know you needed to know the demon's name to fully control it, why would Itsuko know you need magic?"

"Shit! You might well be right. If she opens it, Vorgon is apt to go on a rampage. Even without his true name, Cristo would've been able to exert some influence over the demon." He shook his head. "A completely unbound elder demon is pretty close to my worst nightmare."

They'd barely gone five miles when Daisuke spotted a tan van on the side of the road. He had no time to say anything before Natsumi pulled off the road and parked behind it.

As soon as they got out she drew Flame Edge. Daisuke pointed at the driver's side. She nodded and he moved around to the passenger side.

What he found was a body lying in the ditch. The guy was dressed in tan coveralls and had on heavy work boots. A farmer or mechanic most likely. Daisuke only needed a quick glance to tell that his life force was gone and from the look of his neck, Itsuko had broken it. Talk about bad luck.

"There's no one here," Natsumi said.

"No one living anyway. I've got a body over here. Could you give your new friends on the local police force a call?"

She came around, took one look at the dead man, and ran back out of sight. Daisuke patted the body down and soon came up with a wallet. His driver's license was visible through a clear plastic window.

He pulled out his phone. "Boss, looks like they switched vehicles. Can you find out what kind of car Akira Soma drove?"

"Why don't you just ask him?"

"Because someone broke his neck."

"Ah. Hold on."

The line went quiet and Daisuke tossed the dead man's wallet back on his body. They needed to get this wrapped up soon. Hopefully before the body count got any higher.

CHAPTER EIGHTEEN

Itsuko had driven cars, pickups, boats, and even a snow mobile once, but a tow truck was a first for her. Luckily it had all the modern conveniences like automatic transmission and power steering. She just ignored the quartet of hydraulic levers and treated it like a heavy-duty pickup. The most important thing about it at this point was the full tank of gas.

She made a hard right and ignored the honking of the sedan she cut off. No way was she going back into the city. There were too many cops. She'd stick to the back roads and hope Cristo woke up before the Kugos caught up to them.

She stole a quick glance at her master, or partner—Itsuko wasn't exactly sure of the best way to describe their relationship. Cristo was certainly in charge, but he rarely compelled her to do anything through their link and when he did it was usually the right move. Even when she concentrated with all her might she barely felt his presence in the back of her mind.

For the first year of their partnership, she'd resented that constant presence. Now she found it comforting, a reminder that she wasn't alone in the world. No matter what, Itsuko didn't want to go back to being alone.

"Wake up, damn you! You're tougher than this!" He didn't even flinch when she shouted at him. Cristo always hated it when she yelled. "What should I do?"

He hadn't seemed this bad when she first picked him up. Halfway up the driveway of that farm where he planned to hide, Cristo had blacked out completely and hadn't woken up again. Maybe bouncing up that damn dirt track had jarred something inside him. She didn't know and it was driving her nuts.

Her gaze shifted to the bulge in his pocket. She could always summon the demon and make him heal Cristo. That should be a cinch for something as powerful as a demon.

Itsuko latched onto the idea. If Cristo hadn't come to in fifteen more minutes, she'd stop and free the demon. As long as she had the seal, He had to do what she said. Cristo told her the most important thing was to not show any fear and to stay focused on what you wanted the demon to do. The only reason he didn't summon the creature himself was the concern that he'd be too weak in his current state to maintain control.

She might not be a wizard, but you'd never find anyone more determined to get what they wanted.

Daisuke and Natsumi were back on the road after leaving the dead man in the care of the local police force. The cops in this sleepy part of the country weren't terribly pleased with all the chaos. One of them, a gentleman Daisuke guessed had to be at least sixty, informed him in a disbelieving tone that would've been amusing under different circumstances, that their precinct hadn't had a murder in seventy years. Daisuke had been tempted to ask when they had their last wizards' duel, but didn't want to be unkind to the poor guy.

He checked his tracker, but judging from the dim glow, Itsuko had put quite a bit of distance between them. Daisuke felt everything spiraling out of control and he didn't like it one bit.

His phone rang, dragging him out of his thoughts. "I could use some good news, boss."

"I'm not sure how good it is, but your dead man was likely driving a tow truck."

He stared at his phone. "She stole a tow truck? You're kidding."

Why that struck him as completely ludicrous he couldn't have said, but it did. Things just kept getting weirder on this mission.

"That's the good news. The bad news is that we haven't been able to pick them up on any traffic cams. My best guess is that she's avoiding the city."

"That makes sense considering everyone's looking for them. Thanks, boss." He disconnected and turned to Natsumi. "You heard?"

"Yeah. Should be easy to spot them anyway. How many tow trucks could there be around here?"

Given his luck, there'd probably be a tow truck convention in the area.

"Assuming we survive, what are you going to do next?" she asked.

"I'm going to lock the prison up in our vault, then I'm going home for a few days, then I'm sure the boss will have another mission for me. That's pretty much how my life works. Why?"

"Just curious. Think you'll visit Japan again?"

"Not if I can avoid it." She winced and he was surprised to find he felt bad about it. "I don't have a ton of good memories here. Better for everyone if I keep my distance. But of course who knows. Some other idiot museum director might decide to put a dangerous artifact on display."

"Do you think I could join the Circle of Sorcery?"

"You haven't even graduated high school. Besides, why would you want to? You've got a bright future here. In another decade or so you'll be as strong as your father. The Kugo clan has a lot of power and prestige. You'll have a ton of options. I have an apartment I seldom visit, no health insurance, a lousy retirement plan, and a boss whose name I don't even know. My life consists primarily of traveling all over the world fighting lunatics for dangerous magical items."

"I understand that, but it's important work. What the clan does feels... minor in comparison."

"It's not minor to the people you help." He ran a hand through his hair. "Look, finish school and talk to Ryo. If, after you graduate, you want to give it a shot for a year or something, I'll vouch for you. You can call it a gap year with demons."

"Really?" She sounded surprised. "I thought I'd have a harder time convincing you."

"Look, there aren't so many trustworthy people in the magical community that we'd turn one down. You're strong enough to be useful, though I wouldn't send you out on a solo mission. You're also sane enough that we wouldn't have to worry about you stealing something dangerous and going on a rampage." He checked the tracker again. The light was finally growing brighter. "We're catching up. I'd say she's got a mile or so on us. What's up there?"

"No idea. We've been following this windy back road and seen nothing but farms and the occasional home. Seems like there's got to be a town around here somewhere."

"That's what I'm afraid of."

As if on cue, a beam of darkness shot straight up into the air directly ahead of them. Someone had opened the prison.

CHAPTER NINETEEN

When Itsuko finally reached what passed for a town around here, Cristo still hadn't woken up. If anything he looked even worse—his dark skin had taken on a gray tinge and his breathing was so shallow she could hardly see his chest moving. It was time to stop screwing around and call the demon. She'd make the damn thing heal Cristo, one way or another.

She pulled into a parking lot behind the town's only business, a general store that also claimed to sell food. Their culinary delights interested her a good deal less than finding a quiet spot to do what she had to.

A single car sat in the parking lot and no people were visible. That was good enough for her.

Itsuko patted Cristo down and quickly came up with both the prison and the seal. She tried really hard not to think about how cold his body felt.

"Okay, let's do this."

She slipped the seal into the depression on the top of the prison. A vibration ran through her hands.

Every instinct demanded that she toss the prison out of the cab. She fought it since that would mean losing the seal as well. Five seconds after the vibrations began they stopped.

Where the hell was the demon?

She got her answer a second later when a pillar of black energy shot up out of the prison. Shocked but unharmed, she stared up through the hole in the roof. Clouds were gathering and a shape was visible flying among them.

Was the brute ignoring her?

Itsuko slammed the door open and leapt out. She raised the prison over her head and shouted, "I hold the seal, demon! I command you to appear before me!"

Worry and anger warred within her as the demon continued to ignore her commands. The clouds were now so thick that it might as well have been night. People were emerging from their various homes to stare up at the sky.

When Itsuko looked back she found herself face to chest with... something. The black, scale-covered body, six tentacles for arms, and head of a goat certainly argued for this being the demon.

Screams rang out in the street, but she didn't dare shift her focus. "I hold the seal. You must obey me. Heal Cristo."

The demon stared at her for a moment with its inky-black eyes, then he laughed. If evil had a sound, surely that deep, harsh wheeze of a laugh was it.

"Stupid mortal, you aren't a wizard and clearly don't know my name. You can no more command me than you can the sun. As for the human you wished healed, that isn't something demons can do. And even if we could, it's impossible to heal a corpse."

Her knees wobbled when it said Cristo was dead, but she kept her focus. "He was a warlock. Bring his soul back from Hell."

The demon shook his head back and forth. "As mortals go, you seem especially ignorant. I have a minute before my servants finish claiming the lives of everyone in this town. First, as I said, you don't command me. Second, only a demon lord has the power to return a soul from Hell and even then, you'd have to perform a proper summoning."

Itsuko slumped. Everything had gone wrong. Now that the demon had pointed it out, she could finally tell that the ever-present link was gone. Cristo really was dead.

"What happens now?"

"Now I'm going to wring the life from this miserable country and summon an army of demons in the process. Once I'm done, I'll conquer this world for my master. Not that you'll be here to see it."

Something cold slammed into her back and slithered into her body. Everything went numb and when she lost awareness, she found she welcomed oblivion.

D ay had turned to night and the clouds continued to spread. Natsumi wasn't sure what was going on, but the spirits were screaming in the back of her mind and it was taking all her focus to keep the car on the road. The black column they'd seen earlier was gone, but nothing seemed to have improved.

"Well, we've completely failed," Daisuke said. "Vorgon is free and has already begun summoning his army."

"How do we stop him? The spirits are shouting for me to do something."

"The only way to stop him is to find the prison and the seal and force Vorgon back inside."

"That sounds simple enough."

"Doesn't it? Pity it's probably the most difficult thing I've had to do in my life to this point." Daisuke held up the tracker for her to see. The light had completely gone out. "She's dead. Vorgon probably killed her and used her body to host a demonic spirit as soon as she opened the prison."

Natsumi had trouble feeling bad about that.

They were a hundred yards outside of town when a group of people came running toward them. Natsumi slowed a fraction.

"Run them over."

"What?"

"They're thralls now. Even if you hit them it won't kill them, but it might slow them down. Floor it."

She grimaced but did what he said. When they were close enough she saw the black, dead eyes, distended, fang-filled mouths, and hands ending in long, rending talons.

They hit the first one and it went flying.

The second thrall braced itself and forced them to slow before finally going down.

Three more leapt at the car.

One landed on the hood and punched through the windshield.

Daisuke hit it with a burst of black lightning that sent it flying.

Another ripped open the roof.

She blasted it in the face with crimson flames.

The front end went up and they were at a dead stop.

"Time to go." Daisuke leapt out and sent streams of black lightning in every direction.

Natsumi grabbed Flame Edge and scrambled across the center console to emerge from the passenger side behind him.

She drew and sliced the arm off an approaching thrall. Her second cut removed its head.

When no more enemies presented themselves, she spun and found the remaining demons writhing on the ground, black steam rising off them. A quick glance at Daisuke revealed that his eyes had turned red and the black pentagrams were back.

He kept glaring at the demons until they'd been reduced to ash.

"Are you okay?" he asked.

"Okay enough. I thought that trick was anti-spirit magic."

"It is. Magically speaking, demons and spirits are basically the same."

"Demons and spirits are nothing alike. Spirits are a natural part of the world. Demons are... demons."

"If you say so. We don't exactly have time for a deep philosophical discussion here. Contact the other master clans and let them know what's happening. They'll need to work together to destroy as many demon spirits as possible. When you're done, deal with the other locals. As long as you have Flame Edge you shouldn't have much trouble with a bunch of thralls."

"I don't have the other clan heads' numbers. And what about you?"

"If you don't have their numbers, call Mom. She'll either know them or know where Yoshikazu keeps their numbers. I'm going to find the prison and seal. Solomon's magic won't let a demon touch them which means they have to be around here somewhere."

Natsumi stared at him. Her brain had locked up. It was too much. Her father could've handled this, but she'd just started summer vacation a couple days ago. "I can't—"

"You can and you will. Because if you don't, lots of innocent people are going to die. That cloud represents Vorgon's power and everything it covers will be in danger of demonic possession not to mention high winds, lightning, and rain. Think hurricane from hell. As an elder demon, he can probably summon and maintain a minimum of ten thousand thralls. It'll take time for him to fully recover from his imprisonment, so the faster we can do this the better."

"Ten thousand." She barely breathed out the words. With a shake of her head she stiffened her resolve. "I'll handle it. Go."

Daisuke grinned and raced into the village without hesitation. Natsumi had always considered herself brave, but now she wasn't so sure.

Well, brave or not, she had to save as many people as she could. First, she asked the spirits to keep watch for any approaching thralls then she pulled out her phone.

Aunt Kiyoko picked up on the second ring. "What's happening? The blackest cloud I've ever seen is headed this way."

Natsumi explained the situation. "I need the numbers for the other clan heads."

"They won't listen to a teenage girl. I'll handle them. You help Daisuke. From the sounds of it he knows how to clean this mess up."

She wanted to argue, but her aunt was right. The clan heads were all men in their forties and fifties. No way would they pay any attention to her.

"Okay, I'll leave it to you. Make sure they understand how bad the situation is."

"I'll be very clear. Don't worry, I've met them all and their wives. I can handle this."

Natsumi pocketed her phone and offered a heartfelt

prayer to the spirits that Aunt Kiyoko would succeed and do so quickly.

Now to catch up to Daisuke. She scanned the street ahead of her, but there was no sign of him.

Where had he gone?

CHAPTER TWENTY

Daisuke let out a long sigh as he moved away from their car. If anyone had heard or seen his reaction to heading into a village filled with people that had certainly been transformed into thralls, they would've thought him mad. His relief came mainly from leaving Natsumi behind.

It wasn't that he didn't trust her. The truth was that over the last few days he'd come to like and trust her very much. The problem was that she lacked both the experience and raw power to be much help in a situation like this. Fighting by himself freed him from having to worry about her and let him focus on the task at hand.

Speaking of the task at hand, a pair of thralls darted out from behind a cottage at the edge of the village and lunged toward him.

A burst of black lightning knocked them backwards before his follow-up spell reduced them to ash. He ground his teeth, but there was nothing to be done for these unfortunate people. They were already dead. Their bodies were just being used to house demonic spirits.

Hopefully Vorgon wouldn't want to waste the power needed to summon proper demons. That would up the difficulty of his task considerably.

I found the prison, Master. It's behind the store near the center of the village. The thieves are guarding it.

Since his tracker had already confirmed Itsuko's death, they must've been transformed. No way would Vorgon leave a pair of thralls to guard the prison. Whatever they'd been turned into, Daisuke had no doubt he would be in for a far harder fight than anything he'd faced so far.

He blasted another pair of thralls on his way to the rear of the store. He'd expected to have to deal with a whole mob of the ugly things. That was about all thralls were good for after all. Where could the other villagers be?

Dismissing the pointless question with a shake of his head, Daisuke stepped into the parking lot. The bronze prison sat on the ground while Itsuko and Cristo stood on either side of it. Their eyes glowed red, which confirmed that at least greater spirits had been summoned to inhabit their bodies. Even more interesting, the demons hadn't altered their host corpses. The pair could've been normal humans if not for the eyes.

Since they made no move to attack, he took a moment to cast defensive spells. The simple shield that always surrounded him got a power-up. Next, he added fire and lightning barriers. They wouldn't stop a direct hit, but would protect him from glancing blows. Finally he sent ether into his body, making it stronger and faster by several orders of magnitude.

And that was all the power he dared expend on defense.

Daisuke conjured black lightning around his fingers and charged with enough force to crack the pavement.

Three strides from the prison, the demons finally reacted.

Cristo sent a hellfire blast his way.

Daisuke slid under the crimson and black flames and lashed out at Itsuko who had sprinted towards him.

Black lightning slammed into her chest and sent her flying hard enough to embed her body in the tow truck door.

As soon as the stream of hellfire stopped, he sprang to his feet and sank a lightning-enhanced fist into Cristo's stomach.

Destructive magic rushed out, blowing him across the parking lot and through the wall of the general store.

Master!

Daisuke didn't think.

He dropped to his knees an instant before Itsuko's foot passed through the space his head had just occupied.

The demons were using their host bodies' natural abilities and enhancing them with corrupt ether. If he'd needed more proof that he was dealing with greater demon spirits, that would have cinched the matter for him.

Before Itsuko could recover from the kick, he lashed out with one of his own to her knee.

He might as well have tried kicking a tree for all the good he accomplished. Even his enhanced strength wasn't enough to let him damage her.

Hardly surprising, but it wouldn't have hurt his feelings to catch a break.

The other one is getting up.

Daisuke did a backwards roll and came to his feet.

Necrotic energy shot out, rotting all the store's supports and sending the entire building crashing down on Cristo.

That should buy him half a minute.

Itsuko's fist crackled with lightning as it rushed toward his face.

Daisuke turned away, but not enough.

The blow grazed his cheek and staggered him a step. The world spun for a moment, but at least the lightning shield held.

He dodged a left and ducked a kick.

Snarling his annoyance, Daisuke activated Crimson Haze. Ether flowed into his eyes and they started to burn.

As did Itsuko. She collapsed as the demon inside was slowly obliterated by his spell.

It took longer than the thrall earlier, but at last nothing remained of her but ash.

He'd barely released the spell when a blast of hellfire slammed into his side and sent him skidding across the parking lot. His back screamed, but long years of fighting allowed him to block out the worst of it.

Cristo had finally dug himself out of the store and was lining up another blast.

Daisuke's black lightning lanced out first, sending Cristo toppling over backwards and his hellfire spraying into the sky.

Are you okay?

No, but I'll live. How about a little warning next time?

I tried but your focus on Crimson Haze wouldn't let me through.

That was the other bad thing about that spell. It took so much focus to defeat a powerful foe that he grew oblivious to everything around him.

Done was done. Now he needed to finish off Cristo.

Daisuke summoned the black disk under the former warlock and black lightning shot up. Each bolt burned away a chunk of flesh along with the demonic essence residing in it.

Cristo tried to fight his way out of the circle forcing Daisuke to add a barrier element to lock him in place.

The constant casting was wearing him down. Maybe he should've taken the time to grab his staff.

Clenching his jaw against the building backlash headache, Daisuke forced more ether into the spell.

A final, massive bolt of black lightning blew Cristo into charred lumps of flesh.

Daisuke sat down hard and let out a breath. He barely had time to draw another one before a summoning circle appeared and a true demon rose out of it. The beast stood on two legs and was covered in black, chitin-like armor. It carried a kris-bladed longsword made of the same material.

Daisuke had just time enough to wonder how he was going to deal with this thing when the circle vanished and the demon took a step toward him.

Natsumi walked slowly down the street toward the silent village. A shiver ran up her spine. She'd never felt anything like this. Everything was wrong. The spirits had fallen silent and that actually worried her more than their earlier screaming. It was like they'd given up.

At least Flame Edge was still burning bright. She needed the light as it seemed to be getting darker by the moment. A quick glance up at the clouds confirmed that Vorgon was still flying around up there. That was fine with her. Natsumi might not know exactly how powerful an elder demon was, but she doubted she'd last a heartbeat in a fight with one.

When her gaze shifted back, she found a dozen shambling figures in the street and more emerging from the various houses all the time. They looked like zombies at first, but when one of them looked her way, it crouched like a sprinter on the line then exploded toward her at a dead run.

Long claws flashed at her face.

Natsumi countered with Flame Edge, cutting the thrall's arm off at the elbow.

It showed no sign of pain as it instantly attacked again with its other arm.

She removed that one as well along with its head a second later.

The rest of the monsters offered her no chance to celebrate her victory. Where one had fallen, she now found herself facing off against a dozen more.

These were no honorable opponents and they came at her in a rush.

At her mental command the spirits created a wall of fire in front of her.

One of the monsters barreled right through it, emerging smoking but largely unscathed.

An overhead chop bisected its head and sent it crashing to the ground.

That was two down.

Another one leapt through the flames while its comrades circled around.

Natsumi was forced to retreat or end up surrounded.

She grimaced and cut down another thrall. They weren't all that tough, at least not to Flame Edge, but there were so many of them. This was going to take forever and she doubted she had that long.

A loud crack sounded deeper in the village. She'd heard that often enough to know that Daisuke had found someone to fight.

The thralls were coming from both sides of the wall of fire now. They didn't seem to be in any rush to fight her. That was strange considering how aggressive the earlier one was.

Were they trying to delay her so she couldn't help Daisuke? She wouldn't have thought them smart enough, but now she wasn't sure.

Either way, time was running out.

Natsumi dispelled the wall of fire and sent ether into the blade, enhancing the flames until they burned nearly blue. This spell would tire the sword spirit, but she needed to get rid of the thralls quickly.

When it felt like the sword was on the verge of exploding, she made a horizontal slash and released the gathered energy. "Flash Cut!"

A giant curved blade of flames arced out, slicing the thralls in half and making a clear path.

She sprinted down it, ignoring both the still-thrashing thralls and the now-far-dimmer flames surrounded her blade. As long as the flames didn't vanish altogether, the spirit still had strength enough to fight.

The loudest crack yet sounded, drawing her attention toward the largest building in town as it slowly collapsed.

She shook her head and tried not to think about how much damage they were doing. It wasn't like there was anyone still alive to complain.

Natsumi ran into the parking lot behind the store just in time to see a massive demon covered in shiny black armor emerge from a portal. It carried a wavy bladed sword and took a step toward Daisuke who was getting slowly to his feet. He looked exhausted.

He couldn't possibly beat the demon in the shape he was in now.

Steeling herself, Natsumi rushed past him and swung Flame Edge with all her might.

The demon blocked her strike with its own sword seemingly with ease.

A flick of its wrist sent her flying ten feet back where she landed beside Daisuke.

"What is that thing?" she asked.

"Exactly what you think it is, a true demon. It appeared after I destroyed Cristo and Itsuko. I suspect Vorgon left it behind as a final line of defense."

"How do we stop it?"

"Excellent question. I'm not sure we can. I used way too much power fighting the other two, and you're just not strong enough." Natsumi glared at him but Daisuke shook his head. "Don't give me that look. You know it's the truth just as well as I do."

She did, damn him. "Why isn't it trying to kill us?"

The demon seemed content to stand where it was and stare at them with its glowing red eyes. Natsumi neither understood nor liked what it was doing.

"Best guess? Vorgon summoned it to protect the prison. As long as we don't attack it or try and take the artifact, it can just stand there and wait. Its master is getting stronger by the minute, which means we don't exactly have time on our side."

"So?"

"We need to figure out if it's bound to a place or to the prison itself. Move to the right and throw a fire blast at it. Be ready to fall back until it stops."

Was he crazy? "What if it doesn't stop?"

"It will. As long as I'm here, it can't leave the prison. Trust me."

Natsumi grimaced but nodded and started edging around

to the demon's right. It kept a close watch on her, but every once in a while darted a look at Daisuke just to make sure he hadn't moved.

As she got ready to attack, Natsumi was surprised to find that she did trust Daisuke. Why that surprised her was the bigger question. He'd already saved her life several times and aside from his bad attitude toward the clan, seemed a decent-enough guy.

Her conflicted emotions would keep until later. Gathering fire around Flame Edge, she flicked her wrist and sent a stream of it into the demon.

When the spell ended a few seconds later the demon hadn't so much as flinched.

"You have to hit it like you mean it," Daisuke said.

Natsumi muttered unkind things. That blast had been about three-quarters of her max. If that didn't even get the demon's attention, the only thing she could think to try was Flash Cut.

She tightened her grip on the sword and began condensing ether into it. When she hit her max Natsumi swung Flame Edge with all her will behind it.

An arc of blue-tinged flames shot out and slammed into the demon, staggering it a step.

She had no time to celebrate.

The monster gathered itself and lunged toward her.

Natsumi scrambled back as fast as she could.

It was nearly to her when a blast of black lightning crashed into its side, blowing it ten feet to her right.

"Hit it again!"

Was he crazy? She couldn't use Flash Cut again so soon.

The demon righted itself and loosed a little growl.

If she couldn't use her magic to hurt it, she'd have to do it the old-fashioned way.

She charged and swung her sword.

It blocked the attack easily.

Natsumi darted in and out, avoiding its cuts and getting hers parried in return. It was like fighting her father. No matter what she tried, she couldn't get through its defense.

A rush of power flooded her and her tempo increased.

A cut got through and she actually scratched the demon's armor.

It growled again.

Chill energy slammed into her, freezing her in place.

Fight as she might, Natsumi couldn't move.

The demon's sword went back.

Black lightning sent it sprawling.

The next thing she knew Daisuke was beside her.

He lifted her into his arms and ran toward the back wall of a neighboring building.

Behind them the demon roared like a mad thing.

When they reached the shadow covering the wall, Daisuke ran right into it.

The next thing Natsumi knew they were beside the car. Daisuke set her down and grinned. "Good job."

"Why did you run? I thought you needed the prison?"

The bronze cylinder appeared, seeming to float in midair. A moment later a two-foot-tall humanoid figure with tiny horns, red, scaly skin, and a tail that ended in a stinger like a scorpion's appeared, holding the prison.

"Ruq grabbed it while we kept the demon distracted. Nice work, by the way."

"Piece of cake, Master. I could actually go for some cake right now."

"Focus. First we deal with Vorgon, then you can have a whole cake all to yourself."

"And cookies?"

"Sure, why not. If we're still alive, we'll certainly have earned it."

"What now?" Natsumi asked. "And why didn't the demon pursue us?"

"As to the second question, it was bound to the parking lot. I analyzed the spell while you were playing with it. Now I need to force Vorgon back into his prison."

"You mean we need to force it back."

Daisuke shook his head. "You need to keep your distance. Vorgon wouldn't think twice about using you as a hostage. Anyway, do you even know a flying spell?"

"Do you?" she countered.

"Of course I do. I need to be close enough for him to hear my voice for the magic to work. You should go finish off the thralls in the village. I have to make some preparations before I take off."

"You're just trying to get rid of me."

"Yes. Please take the hint."

She was pretty sure he didn't mean anything bad by it, but the dismissal hurt all the same. Natsumi had thought they were partners in the mission. It seemed Daisuke had other ideas. Not that she could say much given how badly she did against the demon.

"Fine, have it your way." She turned back toward the village. "Good luck."

"You too. And stay clear of the general store. I don't know the exact boundaries of that thing's binding."

She muttered more unkind things but forbore comment. He meant well, she was sure of it, no matter how annoying he was. She kept that thought firmly in mind as she left Daisuke behind.

CHAPTER TWENTY-ONE

Daisuke waited until Natsumi was out of sight before taking the metal card out of his pocket and summoning his trunk. He dug down past his clothes and came out with a six-foot gnarled black staff. He felt stronger the moment he touched it.

"She really didn't want to leave," Ruq said. "When this is over, I suspect you'll be getting another chewing-out."

"At least she'll be alive to yell at me. Hopefully Natsumi will be yelling at my battered but triumphant, still-living body rather than my corpse." He returned the trunk to its pocket dimension and put the card away. The wind had picked up and a few drops of rain spattered against his shield. "The prison."

Ruq handed it over. "You shouldn't joke about such things, Master. If you die, horrible things will happen to me."

"Your concern is touching. No wonder your favorite form is a rat."

Daisuke passed a hand over the prison and sent ether into the seal. "Release."

The bronze disk popped off. Okay, step one complete.

He handed the prison back to Ruq and took the seal. The disk vibrated in his hand. He smiled. It was like the artifact knew it was about to go back where it belonged.

Daisuke touched it to the staff. "By the blood of Solomon that flows through my veins I command you to merge."

The seal melted into the staff and the ether swirled as Vorgon's rune appeared on a suddenly smooth section of the wood about six inches from the top. And that finished step two. The easy part was done, now for the tricky bit: compelling the elder demon back into the prison. Daisuke would very much have liked to test the process out on one of the weaker demons, but how did that saying go? Wish in one hand, shit in the other, and see which one filled up first?

"You should've used the staff to begin with," Ruq said.

"Sure, traveling around Kurisato with a black staff wouldn't draw any unwelcome attention. Any wizard that saw it would instantly recognize its power. The less intelligent ones might even try and steal it even though it would do them no good. Or worse, they might try and sell it to Solomon the Great. If that lunatic got his hands on a second piece of the regalia, we'd really be in trouble."

"It's not like he could use it while it was still bonded to you," Ruq pointed out.

"True, but that just means he'd try that much harder to kill me. No, better for my health and wellbeing if I keep the staff on the down-low as much as possible. Give me that. I've got an elder demon to imprison. You keep your distance as well."

"Have no fear on that regard, Master." Ruq handed over the prison.

Ruq might sound like a self-centered coward, but when the chips were down, Daisuke had no doubt that his familiar would be there to help. In this instance, unfortunately, if he needed help, they were doomed.

Daisuke made a circle over his head with the staff and ether rushed into him. His feet lifted off the ground and he willed himself toward the shadowy figure of Vorgon, who was busy circling and expanding the storm. One advantage of leaving the guardian demon alive was that, hopefully, Vorgon wouldn't realize that the demon had failed its mission.

It was a thin hope, Daisuke understood that, but at this point even the tiniest advantage had to be grasped.

A demon spirit that looked a bit like a humanoid shadow flew toward him only to get blasted to nothing when it hit his barrier. Unlike a normal human, it would take a great deal more than a simple demon spirit to kill Daisuke.

Half a mile out, he finally got a good look at Vorgon. Black scales, tentacles for arms, and a goat head. As demons went, he had a pretty conventional appearance. Of course, like Ruq, Vorgon could choose to look like whatever he wanted.

The rain, both of water and demon spirits, got thicker the closer Daisuke got to Vorgon. The wind howled, forcing him to spend power he couldn't afford to lose just to make forward progress. Though the demon spirits still couldn't penetrate his shield, each blow made him wince. The corruption filling the air turned his stomach and it took all his focus not to vomit. This was probably as close to visiting Hell as a living man could get.

Daisuke shook his head. If ever he'd earned a bonus on a mission, this was it.

Vorgon finally took note of his approach a quarter mile out. The demon banked and soon they were face-to-face.

It would never work, but Daisuke figured he'd start out

reasonably. "Could I convince you to get back in the prison? It will be less painful for you if you enter willingly."

Vorgon's harsh, braying laugh was like nails on a chalkboard to Daisuke's soul. "It seems this is my day to deal with ignorant mortals."

"I take that as a no. So be it." Daisuke leveled the staff and chanted. "By my will and the power of the seal be bound. By the blood of Solomon and might of the Staff of Law, Vorgon be bound in bronze."

Chains of pure ether shot out of the prison and wrapped around Vorgon.

The demon roared and thrashed.

His tentacles shattered chain after chain.

Daisuke's soul screamed as each one broke, but he ignored the pain and focused.

As soon as one chain broke another appeared to take its place.

Inexorably Vorgon was drawn closer.

The stench of brimstone and corruption gagged him.

A tentacle snaked out at Daisuke, but he was protected by the binding spell and it only bounced off an invisible barrier.

"Stop! Please! I beg you. Command me and I will serve. I can make you a god among men. With my power you can rule the world. Isn't that what all you humans want?"

"The sane ones don't." Daisuke sent more ether into the staff.

The binding chains grew thicker and glowed brighter. More emerged from the prison until Vorgon was wrapped head to toe and looked like a mummy.

White light surrounded the demon and then shrank to the size of a roll of coins. The tube of light slid into the prison.

Daisuke let out a breath. He hurt everywhere, though the

worst pain was spiritual rather than physical. But that was only step three done. Now for the fourth.

He raised the prison over his head and tapped it with the staff. A pure, deep chime sounded. Nodding to himself, Daisuke began spinning the staff.

A tornado of white light sucked the darkness and corruption into Vorgon's prison. Demon spirits screamed as they were absorbed. It was like a tornado of the damned and he was at the center of it.

Insulated by the staff, he rode the waves of evil, buffeted but untouched.

He lost all sense of time, but eventually the screams and darkness vanished.

Finally, now for the last step. "Darkness bound in bronze, blood compels and the staff commands, be sealed away for all time."

A final tap of the staff closed up the hole in the top of the prison, leaving only a shallow, perfectly round depression on top.

The sun warmed his face and gleamed on the steel and glass of Kurisato's towers. The battle was done, for today at least.

CHAPTER TWENTY-TWO

Daisuke woke in a soft bed and with a drum pounding his head. The previous day's—it was just yesterday, right?—events came rushing back. Suddenly everything hurting made more sense. The drum, on the other hand, baffled him.

"It's not a drum," Ruq said. "Someone is once again knocking on our door at an unholy hour, albeit a slightly less unholy hour than last time."

"Oh. Be a good imp and tell whoever it is to go away." He pulled the blanket up over his head, but it didn't do much to muffle the noise.

"Daisuke, open up!" Natsumi said.

"Aw, shit. I saved the country, you'd think she'd let me sleep in."

He threw the blankets aside and finally opened his eyes. Somehow he'd made it back to his hotel room. The fact that he couldn't remember the trip worried him a little, but he chalked it up to exhaustion.

"I guided you, Master. By some miracle you landed only

two blocks from the hotel after defeating Vorgon."

"Good job." Daisuke stood and scratched his tangled hair. His quick glance around revealed no sign of either the staff or the prison.

"You put them both in your trunk," Ruq offered. "There was also mention of cake and cookies…"

"Later. I did see chocolate chip pancakes on the menu. What do you say to a double order?"

"I say yes—"

"Daisuke, come on."

He walked to the door and yanked it open. "What? What in heaven's name are you doing at my door at—" He glanced at the digital clock beside his bed. "Ten o'clock. I guess that's not so bad. Do you want chocolate chip pancakes?"

"No, thank you. I had breakfast three hours ago. Are you okay? What about the demon? Since the weather is back to normal I assume you dealt with it."

"I'm fine if tired and hungry. The demon's back where he belongs. I'm touched that you came to check on me."

"What? No. Uncle Yoshikazu finally woke up. He's asking to speak with you."

"And?"

"And your mother asked me to come get you. Hurry up and get ready."

"I think we've pretty well established that I don't take orders from you or any other member of the Kugo clan. My plans consist of ordering breakfast, taking a shower, eating breakfast, and going home. None of that involves talking to Yoshikazu. Last time I talked with him he forced me to hand over the prison and we both know how that turned out. I'm not eager to try it again."

"Don't forget cake and cookies," Ruq added.

"Right, we'll get those in Zurich at our usual place."

Turning back to Natsumi he said, "It's been interesting. Tell Mom and Shogo goodbye for me." Part of him would've liked to see them in person before he left, but it wasn't worth the stress. "If you still want to work for the Circle, call me next year."

Daisuke went to the door hoping she'd take the hint. Of course, Natsumi didn't move. He looked from her to the open door and raised an eyebrow.

"You can't just leave without saying goodbye."

"Pretty sure I can." Out of the corner of his eye Daisuke spotted Ruq in his rat form climb up on the nightstand and grab the phone.

Good thinking. Heaven knows how long it'll take me to get her out of here.

It might be less troublesome just to agree to go, Master. Part of you wants to.

More of me doesn't. Whose side are you on, anyway?

I'm on the side that gets her on her way so we can eat.

Ruq started ordering and Daisuke swallowed a sigh. "Come back at noon. I'll be ready to go by then."

She shook her head. "You'll just vanish once you're done and I'll never see you again."

"If I say I'm going to do something, then I do it. Now go away so I can get ready."

Natsumi gave him one last searching look then nodded and strode toward the door. She paused just outside. "I'll be back."

"Of that I have no doubt, Princess." He shut the door and rested his head against the cool metal. "I'd rather fight another demon."

"No, you wouldn't. However bad it might be, there's almost no chance that you're going to get killed at your family's home. Demons are a much more dangerous proposition. I got a dozen pancakes along with hash browns and bacon."

Daisuke's mouth watered. All the casting he did yesterday left him starving as well as exhausted. "What about hot chocolate?"

"An extra large."

"Are you sure you're an imp and not an angel?" Daisuke grinned and headed for the bathroom. If he was going to have to deal with his family, at least he'd do it clean and buzzing from a sugar high.

A t noon exactly Natsumi returned to pound on his door. This time Daisuke was dressed, fed, and ready to go home. He'd also updated the boss and told her to expect him for breakfast. He deserved two breakfasts after the day he had yesterday. A brief stop at the Kugo estate wouldn't delay him that much and he resolved to put in an appearance, smile and nod, and get out as quickly as possible. Happily, now that he was recovered, getting out would only involve a step through the nearest shadow.

As they bounced up the road to the estate in the red SUV he'd spotted on his first two visits, Natsumi kept flicking glances his way. After the fourth time he asked, "What are you looking at?"

"You're not going to get into an argument with Uncle Yoshikazu are you? He's only been awake for a day and too much stress wouldn't be good for him."

"There's nothing he could say that I care enough about to get angry over. As long as he doesn't do something stupid like demand I return the prison to his dubious protection, we'll be fine. Are you getting your car fixed?"

"It's totaled. I'm not looking forward to filling out the insurance paperwork, I can tell you that. Torn apart by demon thralls. How do you even categorize such a thing? Certainly not an act of god. Natural disaster? There was nothing natural about those things. By the way, I ended up cutting down over a dozen more before the rest collapsed."

"When I bound Vorgon, I pulled the demon spirits he summoned, as well as the true demon we fought, into the prison with him. They're all mushed together in a giant blob of corrupt energy. I hope they're absolutely miserable."

Both checkpoints waved them through and the next thing he knew they were walking across the yard to the main house. Ruq flew silent and invisible at his shoulder. On the porch, his mother was standing by the door. She looked beautiful in her red kimono and her hair done up in some fancy style held together with black-lacquered chopsticks.

A few strides from the porch Natsumi said, "I'll leave you here. It's been… something."

"It certainly has. I hope Ryo's doing better. So long." He threw her a wave and marched up to his mother and gave her a hug. "Hey. Do you know what Yoshikazu wants?"

"Couldn't you call him Dad? Just for a little while?"

"No."

She sighed. "Fine, be stubborn. Come on, he's resting in our room. Shogo is with him."

Daisuke kicked his shoes off and followed her through the austere living room and up to the second-floor bedroom his parents shared. She slid the door open and stepped through with him right behind. Yoshikazu was propped up by a mound of pillows. It was strange seeing him in a white robe instead of the usual suit. Though pale, his eyes held the familiar, hard determination. As soon as Daisuke saw that, he knew Yoshikazu would be okay.

Shogo sat in a chair beside the bed. His jeans and t-shirt were rumpled and wrinkly. Dark circles under his eyes attested to just how little sleep he was getting.

"Afternoon, little brother. Yoshikazu, looks like you're going to make it. Congratulations." When no one spoke for half a minute Daisuke asked, "So, why am I here and not back in Zurich?"

"Your mother told me what happened, that you cleaned up the clan's mess. I wanted to thank you for that. I never should've made you return the artifact. That was my mistake. I let honor blind me to the greater good."

Daisuke nodded. Everything Yoshikazu said was correct, but he saw no need to comment. All's well that ends well as they say.

"You're welcome." He looked from his brother to his mother and back to Yoshikazu. "Was there anything else?"

"Given all that you've done for Japan," Yoshikazu said. "I think you've proven that the spirits made a mistake when they rejected you. Assuming the other master clans agree, I wanted to officially welcome you back to the Kugo clan."

"Isn't that awesome!" Shogo blurted the words out like he'd been saving them up. "You won't have to leave. No one will mind now if you live with us."

"I know you mean well, but I have no interest in returning to the clan or Japan for that matter. I'm not sure what you imagine I've been doing for the last ten years, but I've made a life for myself. I've got an apartment, friends, a job. Do you think I'm just going to leave it all behind to come back here?"

Shogo jumped to his feet. "Don't you want to come home?"

Daisuke smiled, but he was sad rather than amused. "This isn't my home, and it hasn't been for a long time. You seem to have turned out okay, Shogo, and I'm glad. You're welcome to visit me in Zurich anytime, assuming you don't mind sleeping on the couch. My apartment only has one bedroom. Natsumi has my number if you want to call. Mom, I'm glad we got to talk. Yoshikazu, take it easy. Later."

So saying he turned toward the door. He was halfway through the living room when his mother caught up to him. "Will you visit again?"

"Doubtful, assuming another demon prison doesn't pop up. I told Shogo he could visit and the offer extends to you. Call, text, or come in person, I'm happy to talk anytime. Love you, Mom." He gave her a final hug and kiss on the cheek.

Daisuke slipped his shoes on and strode across the yard to the deepest shadow covering the side of the garage. Ruq settled on his shoulder and a moment later he vanished into the darkness.

CHAPTER TWENTY-THREE

D aisuke made his way through the morning gloom toward downtown Zurich. This part of the city had an official name, but he never bothered to memorize it since even if he did, he wouldn't be able to pronounce it. He called it "downtown" because it was the part of the city with the most shops and restaurants, including Ruq's favorite bakery. His too if he was being honest.

The Circle of Sorcery's main office was located in the back room of an occult bookstore. It was actually far too small for all the agents to meet at once, but since the bulk of them were usually out on missions, it served its purpose. The front also made it a natural place for wizards to visit, so anyone keeping watch wouldn't be able to tell who was a member and who was a customer.

A chill breeze blew off Lake Zurich, making him shiver. Though early summer had arrived, it was still brisk this morning. All the people out and about at this hour were wearing long sleeves or sweatshirts. Daisuke was the only idiot wearing a t-shirt.

What do you think she'll have for breakfast?

Ruq was staying invisible as they walked. Magic might be well known enough not to draw comment, but an imp, even one bound as a familiar, was still a demon and he made people nervous. That wasn't the effect Daisuke wanted today.

Something healthy I'm sure. You know how the boss is.

Ruq grumped through their link. Healthy eating wasn't high on his familiar's list of pleasures.

Relax, we'll stop at Stein's Bakery on the way back.

My cake and cookies at last.

Ruq had more of a one-track mind than Daisuke. He turned down a side street and soon found himself standing in front of the brick face of Arcane Books and Trinkets. Ignoring the still-locked main entrance, he went around back to the employee's door. Officially, Daisuke was employed in inventory acquisition for the shop.

That was at least sort of true. The fact that they rarely sold any of the stuff he acquired was best not looked at too closely.

He pulled his key out of his pocket and unlocked both the deadbolt and the regular lock. A subtle shift in the ether deactivated the security wards for thirty seconds. He slipped inside and closed and locked the door behind him. The short walk to the boss's office took him past first the bathroom then the stock room.

Before he could knock on the office door, a beautiful blond woman seemed to appear out of nowhere and leapt at him.

He caught Helena, gave her a spin, and set her down. A classic Nordic beauty, Helena had long blond hair, ice-blue eyes, perfect pale skin, and a figure that remained fully undisguised by her thin cocktail dress. She joined the Circle a year before him and they'd gone on a few missions together before he started working solo.

"You're in better shape than I expected," Daisuke said.

"I'm perfectly fine, but you know the boss's rule, you get a full week's rest after any near-death experience. I hear you dealt with Cristo and Itsuko."

"They were thralls at the time, but yes, I dealt with them. I also had a run-in with your countryman, Haakon."

Her lovely face twisted in a grimace. "That piece of shit is not my countryman. I'm from Iceland and he's from Denmark. Did you kill him?"

"Alas, no. He activated an emergency teleportation spell in the nick of time. I swear the son of a bitch has nine lives." Daisuke shrugged. "There's always next time."

Their conversation was interrupted by a muffled female voice. "Daisuke, you can catch up later. Get in here."

"Ruq and I are going for cake and cookies after. Want to come? My treat."

"You're on. Then maybe back to your apartment to relieve some of my boredom."

Daisuke grinned. "I like that plan."

He collected a parting kiss and pushed through the door to the boss's office. She was seated behind her cluttered desk, staring at him with slightly glowing yellow eyes. Today she wore a gray suit that hugged her curves in a most appealing way. Dark hair hung just past her shoulders. If someone pointed a gun at him and said he had to pick who was more beautiful, Helena or the boss, he'd have trouble making up his mind.

The cigarette butts in a glass ashtray gave off a thin

trickle of smoke. Either she'd been here for a while or was especially nervous.

The boss pointed at an empty chair in front of her desk and he sat. "Morning, boss. You're looking especially lovely today."

That was his standard greeting and he meant it every time he said it.

"Best not let Helena hear you say that. The prison?"

He summoned his trunk and started rummaging. "She's not the jealous type. Besides, our relationship is more glad-to-still-be-alive sex than anything serious. Given our line of work, getting close to a colleague isn't very wise. Or so you assured me."

"I doubted you were listening."

"I listen to everything you say." He pulled out the bronze prison and set it on her desk. "There you go, one can of elder demon."

"And the seal is in place?"

He took out the Staff of Law and showed her Vorgon's rune. "Yup, everything is as it should be."

The boss made no effort to touch the staff. It didn't like anyone but him laying hands on it. As long as you didn't try to use it, the reaction would only be a warning chill, but if you tried to channel ether through it, watch out. Daisuke and the staff were bound until he died. Pity, since so many people wanted him dead for exactly that reason.

"There was supposed to be food." Ruq shimmered into view and landed in rat form on Daisuke's lap.

"Oh, yeah, second breakfast."

"You eat too much and I'm not your mother." The boss looked up from studying the prison. "Speaking of your mother, did she know anything about your true father?"

"She said not. Apparently, it was just a drunken fling to spite my grandparents."

"Her memories hadn't been manipulated?"

"Not that I could see. It happened almost twenty-four years ago, so even if dear old Dad did something to her memories, I doubt anyone could tell now. You really think he had some kind of plot in mind beyond hooking up with a pretty, willing girl?"

The boss shook her head. "I don't know, Daisuke. But with someone bearing the blood of Solomon, it pays to assume the worst."

"Well, if he's running a con, it's a hell of a long one." Daisuke put the staff away. "If there's nothing else, I've got a hungry imp and a horny blond in need of attention."

"I'm taking the prison to our vault. I should show you the entrance."

Daisuke shook his head. "Bad idea, boss. As long as I'm doing field work, better for everyone if I don't know where it is."

"I knew you'd say that, but I had to ask. Someday you may need to know where it is, but we can worry about that later. Go have fun. You've certainly earned it."

"Exactly my plan. Later, boss."

Daisuke left the office and went to find Helena. It was good to be home and no mistake.

Haakon woke surprised to find nothing hurting. The boy's magic had injured him worse than anything he'd encountered in a long time. When the opportunity arose, he planned to pay the brat back tenfold.

He sat up and looked around at the empty Hall of Healing. The nine other beds were unoccupied and the healer himself was absent. Uncertain of his next move, Haakon hopped off the bed and found his shirt and helmet sitting on the floor nearby. He put both on and headed for the door.

In the hall outside, a young man in a white robe that marked him as a new initiate in the Blood of Solomon bowed. "Lord Solomon wished to speak with you as soon as you woke, sir."

Haakon had been expecting this conversation, but didn't look forward to it. He'd failed his master and if he got away with no more than a berating would consider himself lucky.

"Lead on."

The boy set out down stone halls that were lit by torches every ten paces. The effect was decidedly medieval. It wasn't for dramatic effect. Castle Solomon was wholly cut off from the modern world. No electricity, no cell phone service, no internet, no nothing that might allow their enemies to find them with modern technology. A very special artifact protected them from magical searches, one so powerful and important even Haakon had never seen it.

As he expected, the boy led him to the meeting room where the high-level members of the group gathered. Today all save one of the ten chairs surrounding the rectangular table were empty.

At the head of the table, Solomon the Great waited. He wore a simple tan robe that burned bright in the ether. It was the Robe of Power, one of the three pieces of Solomon's regalia. A long white beard hung down to the middle of his thin chest while equally white hair hung down an exactly equal distance in the back. Lord Solomon's eyes glowed white as he looked at Haakon.

"Apologies for my failure, Master." Haakon knelt and

bowed his head, ready to accept any punishment his lord deemed fit.

"Rise and sit beside me. Was it our wayward brother that struck you down?"

Haakon hastened to obey and soon settled in the chair to Lord Solomon's left. Only one person dared sit at his right hand and that honor certainly didn't belong to Haakon.

"Yes, my lord."

"Such a shame. Daisuke would make a mighty ally if only he would see reason. I often wonder why the spirit of our honored ancestor chose to guide him to the Staff of Law. I already wore the Robe of Power. Surely that proves that I'm most worthy to wield the staff."

"Without a doubt, my lord." Haakon wasn't sucking up. He believed in Lord Solomon's greatness and wisdom with all his being.

"Perhaps he means it as a test. That we must either overcome or better yet bring into the fold, our lost brother. Something important is about to happen, Haakon. I don't know what or why, but at night the demons sing to me. They beg to be freed so they can serve me in bringing order to this chaotic world. They grow louder and more desperate by the day."

"How may I serve, my lord?"

"I have begun to isolate the voice of one of the demons. Once I have done so, I will know where to find its prison and seal. You will redeem yourself by claiming both."

Haakon's heart raced at the possibility that he might be able to regain his master's trust. "You may depend on me, my lord."

Lord Solomon touched his wrist and offered a benevolent smile. "I know, brother. How could it be otherwise when we all serve the will of our great ancestor?"

Haakon lowered his head at the mention of their ancestor. Just once he would like to hear the spirit of Solomon the Wise. Perhaps once he'd proven himself worthy, the great spirit would reveal himself.

Haakon would do anything for that reward.

Anything.

AUTHOR NOTE

Hello Everyone,

I hope you enjoyed Daisuke's first adventure. I certainly had a lot of fun writing it. And the fun will continue in book 2, A Friend in Need.

While you're waiting for book two to come out, you can find more of my books on my website, www.jamesewisher.com.

Thanks for reading and I'll see you again soon.

James

The Portal Thieves

The Master of Magic

The Chamber of Eternity

The Heart of Alchemy

The Sanguine Scroll

The Dragonspire Chronicles

The Black Egg

The Mysterious Coin

The Dragons' Graveyard

The Slave War

The Sunken Tower

The Dragon Empress

The Dragonspire Chronicles Omnibus Vol. 1

The Dragonspire Chronicles Omnibus Vol. 2

The Complete Dragonspire Chronicles Omnibus

Soul Force Saga

Disciples of the Horned One Trilogy:

Darkness Rising

Raging Sea and Trembling Earth

Harvest of Souls

Disciples of the Horned One Omnibus

Chains of the Fallen Arc:

Dreaming in the Dark

On Blackened Wings

Chains of the Fallen Omnibus

The Complete Soul Force Saga Omnibus

The Aegis of Merlin:

The Impossible Wizard

The Awakening

The Chimera Jar

The Raven's Shadow

Escape From the Dragon Czar

Wrath of the Dragon Czar

The Four Nations Tournament

Death Incarnate

Atlantis Rising

Rise of the Demon Lords

The Pale Princess

Malice

Aegis of Merlin Omnibus Vol 1.

Aegis of Merlin Omnibus Vol 2.

The Complete Aegis of Merlin Omnibus

Other Fantasy Novels:

The Squire

Death and Honor Omnibus

The Rogue Star Series:

Children of Darkness

Children of the Void

Children of Junk

Rogue Star Omnibus Vol. 1

Children of the Black Ship

Children of The End

ABOUT THE AUTHOR

James E. Wisher is a writer of science fiction and Fantasy novels. He's been writing since high school and reading everything he could get his hands on for as long as he can remember.